A Novel

Higher Education

Chronicles of a Dumpster Fire

To Ginny —
Enjoy!

[signature: Dr. Ashley Oliphant]

Dr. Ashley Oliphant

This is a work of fiction. Names, characters, businesses, places, events, locales, and incidents are either the products of my imagination or used in a fictitious manner. Any resemblance to actual persons, living or dead, or actual events is purely coincidental. That said, there is some shit going down in higher education right now, and the world needs to know about it. While the events in this book did not happen, things exactly like this happen every day at institutions all across America. We laugh so we don't cry.

ISBN: 978-1-957723-47-1

Oliphant. Ashley.
Higher Education

Edited by: PJ Brunson and Amy Ashby

Warren publishing

Published by Warren Publishing
Charlotte, NC
www.warrenpublishing.net
Printed in the United States

This book is dedicated to the phenomenal
English professors who shaped my journey:
Dr. Gail McDonald, Dr. Tony Jackson, and Dr. Boyd Davis.

AUTHOR'S PREFACE

*M*y name is Dr. Ashley Oliphant, and after twenty years of college teaching, I recently retired. I have been involved in higher education—as an undergraduate student and a graduate student; a graduate teaching assistant; a writing center co-director; a service center director; an adjunct, an assistant, then associate, then full professor; a program coordinator; and a chair—for the last twenty-four years. I've seen some things.

Some of those things have been transformative and awe-inspiring. There are no adequate words to describe the level of triumph I have seen my students achieve. Other things have been frustrating beyond belief. I think most teachers would agree this stark contrast between exhilaration and despair characterizes their daily existence.

This book was born in my mind the minute I finished writing my first novel, *In Search of Jimmy Buffett: A Key West Revival*, in 2017. The first few pages of that narrative are set at the fictional Clary-Smith University, the academic home of associate English professor Dr. Livie Green. I knew I wanted to return to Livie's story and to Clary-Smith in a prequel because that segment of the narrative was far from finished. However, at the time I needed to take an artistic detour with my mother, Beth Yarbrough, to co-write our book *Jean Laffite Revealed: Unraveling One of America's Longest Running Mysteries*.

Once we went under contract for that book, there was no doubt in my mind what the COVID-19 quarantine summer of 2020 would be about. Admittedly, it took me a few weeks to hear Livie's voice again, but when she finally spoke, it was clear and comforting. Most people who have never written fiction don't know what it's like to have their whole world consumed by characters, to have their days and nights wrapped up in their dialogue and emotions. In 2017 when I concluded *In Search of Jimmy Buffett*, I actually went into a period of mourning, and that word is not an overstatement. It took about six months to let Livie go and to get back to teaching, administrating, mothering, wife-ing, and living. But she never left me completely.

Aside from revisiting Livie, I needed to write this book to sort through all that I was feeling as I stepped away from the classroom, to capture the humor and delight that teaching always delivered, to air a few decades worth of dissatisfactions, and, quite honestly, to detox from the unhealthy aspects of university life.

I am of the belief that we are hard-wired to write the books that are in us all—it's just a matter of whether or not we decide to let them out. For most of the teachers I know, summer is a time of artistic release. May, June, and July always helped me process the previous year and mentally prepare for the coming fall semester. That processing and preparation was always achieved through writing. This book captures the highs and lows of the teaching life, but my guess is that it is going to resonate with all of you, no matter what field of work keeps you busy. We all know these characters and personalities. We do our best to thrive in broken systems. We have all wasted away in dreadful business meetings and fantasized about clothes-lining the speaker who will just not shut up—well, maybe that one was a bit too specific, but you get what I mean.

Now more than ever, the world needs to laugh, and I hope you will find a giggle on every page. Join me, if you will, as we watch our heroine, Dr. Livie Green, face the academic year 2010-2011 with her characteristic fire. These folks should have known better than to get in her way.

Dr. Ashley Oliphant
June 30, 2022

AUGUST

To: AllFaculty
From: McLovelace, Grady
Sent: Mon 8/2/10 3:32 p.m.

Colleagues,

It is with great excitement that I welcome you back to campus as we prepare for the 2010-2011 academic year.

All of our student athletes have returned to the practice field, and I am certain the Clary-Smith Flying Squirrels are going to soar high again this year.

Over the summer months, the deans and I have been hard at work finalizing the university's new mission and vision statements, which we were assisted with writing by the consulting firm of College Retention and Persistence. At our Fall Professional Development Conference in a few days, we will unveil the university's new cutting-edge tagline. I think you are going to be blown away.

I also want to take this opportunity to publicly dispel the rumor going around that the administration is cutting the drama and dance programs. At its core, Clary-Smith is a liberal arts institution, and the drama and dance programs are central pillars of creativity and innovation, inspiring students, faculty, staff, alumni, and community members with their plays and recitals. I assure you that the arts are alive and well at Clary-Smith.

Let's all commit to making this a year full of growth and prosperity.

Yours in Service,
Dr. Grady McLovelace
Clary-Smith University President

August 3, 2010

Clary-Smith Clarion
A Covert Faculty NEWSPAPER

Because higher education is a dumpster fire, and we don't have the budget to buy extinguishers

Colleagues,

It is with great excitement that I welcome you back to campus for another academic year filled with unethical leadership, financial catastrophe, declining enrollments, and reduced academic rigor, all dressed up like painted pigs under the illusion of institutional transparency.

All 456 student athletes (85 percent of our total student population) have returned to campus ready to prioritize their sports over their academics. The administration will ensure that these Flying Squirrels fly extra high this year, as we will overlook their blatant drug use in the dorms in order to keep their asses on your class rosters.

Over the summer, the twenty deans and I did nothing. Literally nothing. We hired another consulting firm (this one with an acronym that reveals exactly what it is [C.R.A.P.]) to produce another $50,000 report that buys me more time in office to "gather data." When your administrative bloat gives you a dean for every 26.75 students on campus, life is pretty damn good. At our utterly useless Fall Professional Development Conference in a few days, we will unveil the university's new tagline. I think you are probably going to want to slit your wrists with the new logo lanyards that we are planning to cut your faculty travel funds to pay for.

I want to take this opportunity to lie through my suspiciously white teeth about the forthcoming elimination of both the drama and dance programs. They're toast. At its core, Clary-Smith is a professional school that values business and the health sciences. We just keep the rest of you around because our accrediting body requires us to have a General Education curriculum.

Let's commit to making this a year where we are all in therapy and actively on the job market.

Yours in Vodka,
Shady McShitface
Clary-Smith University's Chief Knob

Clary-Smith English Department Fall 2010
Course Offerings for Majors

DR. MERYL KAISER	CREATIVE NONFICTION, THE GRAPHIC NOVEL
DR. OLIVIA GREEN	HEMINGWAY AND THE OUTDOORS, AMERICAN LITERATURE II
DR. DENISE MCGILLICUDDY	POSTCOLONIAL LITERATURE
DR. ROGER EUMENIDES	NARRATIVE THEORY
DR. GEORGIANA PONSONBY	JANE AUSTEN, BRITISH LITERATURE I, WORLD LITERATURE II

EVERY FACULTY MEMBER IN THE ENGLISH PROGRAM WILL HOLD AT LEAST EIGHT OFFICE HOURS A WEEK, INCLUDING TWO HOURS OF AVAILABILITY IN THE WRITING CENTER. PLEASE ACCESS YOUR PROFESSORS DURING THEIR OFFICE HOURS TO DISCUSS YOUR ASSIGNMENTS AND GET FEEDBACK ON YOUR DRAFTS.

IF YOU HAVE ANY ENGLISH ADVISING CONCERNS, PLEASE SEE DR. OLIVIA GREEN IN YARBROUGH 216. SHE WOULD BE DELIGHTED TO TALK TO ANY STUDENT INTERESTED IN JOINING THE ENGLISH PROGRAM AS A MAJOR OR MINOR.

August 8, 2010

Clary-Smith Clarion
A Covert Faculty NEWSPAPER

Because higher education is a dumpster fire, and we don't have the budget to buy extinguishers

All deans, chairs, and program coordinators gathered in late July for a "Leadership Retreat." The morning session, led by Board of Trustees Chairman Burke Halperson, was titled "How to Be an Effective Follower" and ended with Halperson being crowned with the moniker "Burke the Jerk" by all the teaching faculty in attendance. His presentation was based on a 1989 article from the Business and Leadership Journal that compared mid-level managers and lower-level employees to sheep who need to learn the tenets of "followership" in order to avoid distracting the real leaders in an organization from doing the important stuff. Following the workshop, faculty were served boxed lunches that included cold-cut sandwiches that had somehow become moist in transit from the deli. With nothing but a bag of plain potato chips and a cookie in their respective bellies, participants embarked upon a LONG afternoon schedule of passive listening and immeasurable boredom.

Word from our well-placed sources indicates that the Fall Professional Development Conference, organized this year by the Dean of Nothingness himself, Dr. Ronald Grim of the Humanities and Sciences, will be an especially crummy experience for all involved due to his notoriously poor planning. He apparently told his administrative assistant, the long-suffering Tammy Jane Hillyer, two weeks ago that she had to "find some presenters—and fast." When pressed by Hillyer to explain what kind of presenters she was to locate, his response was "I don't know—people who can talk about learning and teaching." This could be the year Tammy Jane goes postal and strangles him with the sleeves of one of his own dopey cardigans.

Our apologies to all new faculty members who had to endure New Faculty Orientation led by the hapless Varner Earnhardt. We recognize that all you really wanted was your office and mailbox keys, your copier codes, and access to the online learning system so you could view your rosters, but what you got was a week of presentations from every single unproductive dean we've got. Not to worry. The senior faculty will get you up to speed about the things that matter.

Additionally, the Clarion would like to offer a word of caution to all new faculty members about Dr. Myrick Page, the Dean of Collaboration. In the Yarbrough building, Dr. Page is known as the Dean of Chit Chat because he will plop down in your office unannounced and blabber aimlessly for an hour or more. Because Dr. Page does not pick up on social cues that demonstrate a listener is no longer interested, and because saying you have to go to class doesn't cause him to budge, faculty often find the only way to escape his grasp is to pretend like their tummy hurts and they need to go to the bathroom urgently. Dr. Georgiana Ponsonby in the English program also suggests avoiding eye contact in the hallway if you can manage it.

To: AllFaculty; AllStaff
FROM: Alder, Dutch
SENT: Sun 8/8/10 11:46 a.m.

Hi all,

Due to another budget shortfall, the art program will host a raffle fundraiser to pay for our planned January field trip to the North Carolina Museum of Art to view the Norman Rockwell exhibit. The top three finishers in the 2009–10 student juried art competition have agreed to donate their winning pieces as raffle prizes. Tickets are $2 each and can be purchased from me or any art major on campus.

Dr. Dutch Alder
Clary-Smith Art Department (All of It–It's Just Me)

Welcome to
Clary-Smith's Fall 2010
Professional Development Conference

AUGUST 9-13
CELEBRATING CLARY-SMITH'S NEW TAGLINE:

SHOOT. SCORE. GRADUATE.

AT CLARY-SMITH, YOU ARE ALWAYS IN THE GAME

***

"You guys, save Denise a seat. It's her first day," Livie Green explained as she sat down at the round table with her breakfast. "If we don't and she's late, she'll have to sit at the front table with the sport management people."

"Judging by the new sports balls university tagline, we're going to need the sport management people to explain all the athletic references that are about to infiltrate our marketing materials," said Georgiana Ponsonby as she took another spoonful of her homemade chia pudding, the solution for her mistrust of the buffets that were usually found at such gatherings.

"Oh my God, did you guys see the cheesey basketball station over there in the corner?" laughed Roger Eumenides. "I mean, what in the entire hell?"

"To get your cafeteria lunch ticket, you have to let the admissions department film you saying, 'Shoot. Score. Graduate.' while you make a shot. It's for a recruitment video." Livie had never been more embarrassed to welcome a new faculty member into her university.

Meryl Kaiser scurried up to the table with baby spit-up on her left shoulder and a maxi pad wrapper stuck to the bottom of her loafer. "This day, y'all. How are we going to make it through eight hours of professional development?"

"With the bottle of whiskey I brought home from my Aphra Behn conference in England this summer," Georgiana said proudly.

"Yay, whiskey! Whiskey! Whiskey! Whiskey!" shouted Meryl.

Denise McGillicuddy saw her new colleagues from across the room and came over, thankful they had saved her a spot on this nerve-racking day.

"Welcome, Denise," Livie said with a warm smile. "We're so glad you made it. And you found the breakfast buffet."

"Yes, I did. Happy first day! It feels good to be here and to finally be getting started," Denise said as she put down her things. "I do have a question, though. Don't all look at once. Do you see that gentleman over there in the plaid shirt with the ink stain on the pocket?"

"Sweet, sweet Lord," Georgiana said as she poured whiskey into her coffee cup under the table.

"Who is that?" Denise asked. "I was behind him in the breakfast line, and when we got to the beverages, he opened his tote bag and started chunking orange juice bottles in there. He took at least ten."

"Ah, Professor McJuicington," Roger explained. "He steals beverages when they are free at university events to fill up the mini-fridge in his office."

"Oh dear," Denise said, befuddled.

"That's Jim Culp, tenured sociology professor," Livie clarified. "Hasn't given anything except a multiple-choice test in forty years. Spends entire class periods reading articles from the journal he edits, despite a mountain of student complaints and years of abysmal teaching evaluations. Welcome to the distinguished faculty at Clary-Smith University, Doctor McGillicuddy."

***

"All right, let's settle in for our first group activity of the day," said Dr. Ronald Grim as the faculty sat down to eat their breakfast. "I am very excited to announce that we have a special consultant here to help us strategize, learn, and thrive through the many challenges facing Clary-Smith University this academic year. Doctor Hamad Arnoud, from the firm Arnoud and Associates in Portland, Oregon, is an industry leader in the field of higher education professional development. In his work with Arnoud and Associates, he has assisted more than one hundred organizations realizing their full potential and navigating troubled waters. Please welcome Doctor Hamad Arnoud."

[Very weak applause accompanied by the resounding scream of an ultra-loud default setting ring tone that Dr. Culp forgot to turn off. It continues as Arnoud makes his introduction because Culp cannot find the phone in his bag beneath all that juice.]

"Thank you, Clary-Smith," Arnoud began. "Oh golly, this is a good-looking group of lifelong learners. I can just feel the pulse of your energy. I can sense your passion. Your commitment to Clary-Smith is absolutely palpable in this space. Let's all take a quiet moment to acknowledge and appreciate that."

GEORGIANA
Today's the day. This is it.
I'm going to lose my shit in
this very meeting.

LIVIE
This man is going to test my Jesus.

"That was so meaningful. Thank you for joining your heart with mine for a moment," said Arnoud as he transitioned over to his laptop. "This beautiful Monday morning is full of promise. We have a blank slate laid before us, and I really sense that we should use this time to solve problems together. We are going to accomplish that by beginning with a collaborative word cloud. My research has found that the process of building a word cloud actually has a simultaneous benefit of building community. Let's build community today, Clary-Smith! Pull out your phones. Humor me on this. Get your phones and put on your thinking caps. Here is the issue: your university has terribly outdated and unreliable technology, and the institution has no money to address the problem. Considering this lack of funding, what do you think the solution to the problem is? And this is the fun part. You are only allowed to answer using one word. Use the link I just emailed to enter your one-word solution to the problem. Go!"

MERYL
So we are going to address a major budget shortfall linked to a long-term infrastructure weakness with one-word answers?

GEORGIANA
I should be working on my syllabi. I should be working on my syllabi. I should be working on my syllabi.

DENISE
We paid to fly him here
to build a word cloud?

ROGER
I just checked Hotwire. A
round-trip ticket from Portland
to Raleigh averages $1,350.

LIVIE
That's double our department's
operating budget. And that
was just for his flight. Who
knows what we paid him as
a speaking fee.

GEORGIANA
I should be working on my syllabi. I
should be working on my syllabi. I
should be working on my syllabi.

DENISE
Is this what they always
have faculty do the week
before classes start?

LIVIE
Yes, each year a different
dean is tasked with putting
together a week of mind-numbing
programming that keeps us away
from writing our syllabi, registering
students for classes, and handling the
hundreds of emails in our inboxes.
It's Clary-Smith's way of saying
"welcome back, gang."

DENISE
At my previous institution, the
first full week was dedicated to
pedagogical training and truly
important planning meetings. I
loved it because I always learned
so much from hearing what my
colleagues were doing in their
classes. So we just sit here
and listen?

MERYL
No, that's not what's ever going to
happen here. Indeed, we do sit here
and listen. It truly boggles my mind.
You have 100 of the smartest people
in the zip code all in one place as a
captive audience. We could REALLY
DO SOMETHING, and yet, we are
put into small groups to complete
mindless tasks that yield nothing.

GEORGIANA
Maybe we should suggest
promoting technological
regression as the next big
thing. Perhaps it might catch on
everywhere, and we would be
national best practices leaders.

ROGER
"Technological regression"
is two words, Ponsonby.
Follow the rules, man.

"Okay team Clary-Smith, let's see what we have created together," Arnoud said with exaggerated excitement. "How do we correct IT's outdated and unreliable technology with no budget? The most popular answers will show in the word cloud ... now."

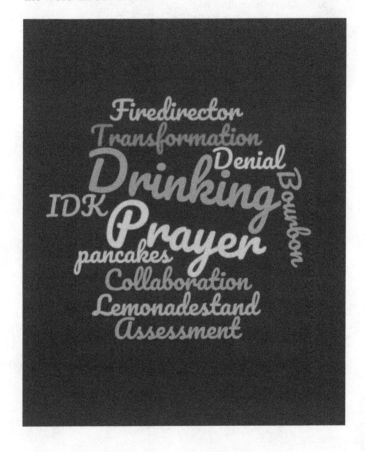

To: All Humanities and Sciences Faculty
From: Grim, Ronald
Sent: Mon 8/9/10 5:04 p.m.

Colleagues,

Thank you for participating in such a productive first day back. Dr. Arnoud was so impressed with your engagement and collaborative spirit. Tomorrow there is another big day on tap for us. During the morning breakfast session, representatives from the firm College Retention and Persistence in Sacramento will lead us in a brainstorming activity designed to facilitate their work on the revision of the university's strategic plan. Come prepared to grow and share.

The Provost also wanted me to announce a new initiative that I think you will find very beneficial. One of the preliminary findings from the initial College Retention and Persistence S.W.A.T. analysis is that the university is not doing enough to increase faculty and staff participation in preventative health care measures. Very soon you will begin to notice a series of emails from Health Services informing you about ways you can stay healthy. I also hear nurse Keesha Forsythe has arranged for some entertaining activities that will help us improve our overall health. Stay tuned!

Dr. Ronald Grim
Dean of Humanities and Sciences, Clary-Smith University

MERYL
Well, there is nobody more
qualified to write the document
that identifies the most pivotal
institutional qualities that
define our culture than a group
of complete outsiders from
California.

LIVIE
I heard from someone
on the finance committee that we
paid them $35,000 to facilitate a
day's worth of information gathering
sessions and then compose a
20-page strategic plan.

ROGER
We are on the wrong end
of this business.

LIVIE
I also heard that C.R.A.P. got
caught selling the same tagline to
two different universities five years
apart. President McShitface knew
and hired them anyway. His former
fraternity brother founded the
company so ... cronyism.

GEORGIANA
Denise, we are so happy you
joined our department, but
we are also so sorry that the
institution's dysfunction is on
display on such a grand scale
this early in your employment.

DENISE
I am happy to be here, though
I have to admit I did not think I
would have to shoot a basketball on
camera to have access to lunch.

To: AllFaculty
FROM: Forsythe, Keesha
SENT: Tue 8/10/10 8:55 a.m.

Clary-Smith faculty,

Did you know that just 20 jumping jacks a day can reduce your risk factor for heart disease by 7%? Jumping jacks are a powerful exercise tool that can help boost your heart rate and stretch important muscle groups (like your shoulders) that are sometimes neglected by people who typically work in office environments. Let's all make it our goal to do 20 jumping jacks a day to stay fit, Clary-Smith!

To Good Health,
Keesha Forsythe, RN
Clary-Smith School Nurse

GEORGIANA
I have exactly 131 unanswered student emails in my inbox because I have to attend these stupid workshops. Please tell me the school nurse didn't just add one about jumping jacks.

ROGER

***

"Well, here we are. How many sports metaphors will it take to create enough weight to crush our spirits on this glorious Tuesday?" In the shower this morning, Livie had promised herself she would stay positive if for no other reason than to help Denise integrate. She was already missing the mark.

"I don't know," Roger said. "Let's ask the magic word cloud generating software. Or did that wizard already fly back to Portland?"

"Sticky notes. I see sticky notes on all the tables," Georgiana said with alarm in her voice. "I am not writing my fucking feelings on a sticky note and sticking it to the wall in a public place again. I will not do it."

"Am I missing something?" Denise asked, genuinely puzzled.

"At our spring faculty conference, that particular consultant, who we paid too much, made us participate in a three-hour 'processing' session designed to engage all of our senses as we explored the issue of racial inequity," Meryl explained. "The sticky notes were obviously the tactile component."

"He played The Notorious B.I.G.'s *Ready to Die* album in the background to engage the aural learners," Roger said while snorting with his giggle. "It was highly inappropriate, completely tone-deaf, and totally hilarious."

"I had to write how I felt on a tiny piece of paper, and then we covered the walls with said tiny pieces of paper and patted ourselves on the back for addressing deep-seeded race-related disparities," Georgiana offered. "Writing our feelings erased three hundred years of racial oppression and violence—just like that."

"Then in the afternoon session, the second consultant taught us how to incorporate Facebook into our classroom activities," Meryl added. "He claimed that 'all the kids were using it these days.'"

"We spent a whole hour just getting everybody logged in for the first time," Livie remembered. "Then a few weeks later, Professor Kip Arthur—a library science professor who passed away mid-semester at the age of ninety-two a few months ago, God rest his soul—used his fledgling technological skills to post that series of unfortunate hammock pictures in which he was wearing nothing but a straw hat and a loose Speedo bathing suit. Many, many students complained, and that's when the board implemented our 'no friending students on social media' policy."

"He was teaching at ninety-two?" Denise asked in total disbelief.

"There were pubes. So many pubes," Meryl said, trying to resist the flashback.

"I can't talk about old man short and curlies or sticky notes while I eat breakfast. Just stop," Georgiana said. With the bottle of English whiskey emptied during the previous day's festivities and nobody thinking to bring more today, the realization set in that they were all going to have to face another day of meetings while stone-cold sober.

***

"Happy day two!" said Dr. Grim. "Welcome back for another day of conferencing that I know you are going to find enlightening and productive. We will make it to the finish line as a winning team!" Just then, Grim's introduction was interrupted by the resounding scream of the ultra-loud ringtone of Dr. Culp's phone. They had all been in enough faculty meetings with Culp the Gulp to expect it.

"As you know, this week we are celebrating Clary-Smith's new tagline—Shoot. Score. Graduate.—which is a product of the hard work of the consultant team from College Retention and Persistence," Grim continued. "We know this new tagline will resonate with our student population and propel them to go for the goal in their own lives. The dean of strategic planning, Doctor Orum Saunders, felt that the best way to launch our new tagline campaign was to produce SWAG. That stands for 'Stuff We All Get.' So, if you will look under your chairs in your gift bags, you will see that you all get a fun surprise!"

MERYL
What in the living HELL am
I supposed to do with a
full-size basketball?

DENISE
Does your administration often
hand out toys to the faculty?

GEORGIANA
Yesterday I went to the business
office supply room, and the
attendant wouldn't give me
a box of staples because the
academic budgets are frozen
until we see how many students
return for fall. We don't have
money for fundamental office
supplies, but we are flush with
cash for basketballs.

ROGER
Basketballs that say "Shoot. Score.
Graduate." in Clary-Smith colors.

MERYL
Are we allowed to throw these
at the basketball players when
they fall asleep in the back row
of our classes?

GEORGIANA
Do you think the business office
would barter a basketball for
a box of staples? This thing
has to be worth $30.

DENISE
Another question. Did Dr. Grim
say the university has a Dean
of Strategic Planning? I thought
we hired a consultant firm for
strategic planning.

LIVIE
That's right, Denise. Dr. Orum
Saunders's entire job is strategic
planning for the institution. Our
current strategic plan has not
been significantly revised in eleven
years under his tutelage. We have
deans for literally everything you
can imagine: Dean of Teaching,
Dean of Learning, Dean of
Collaboration, Dean of Assessment,
Dean of Experiential Learning,
Dean of Service Learning, Dean of
Compliance, Dean of Technological
Innovation. There are twenty in
total, all with full-time administrative
assistants, no teaching load, and
exorbitant salaries.

MERYL
This is what they refer to in the
business as "The Bloat."

LIVIE
This is kind of a baby hamsters situation.
Administrators beget administrators, so the
more of them you have, the faster they multiply.

GEORGIANA
The important thing to remember is that you
can't expose them to light or feed them after
midnight, or they will ransack your town.

LIVIE
Now keep in mind, it is hard work deaning.
Every day you have to schedule a number
of meetings that maintain the mirage of
you actually doing something, in addition to
getting the people below you to write reports
that you can pass off as your own work. They
need the support of consultants when the time
comes to actually produce something tangible.

MERYL
Our Humanities and Sciences dean is a
completely inept turd salad sandwich.
His assistant, Tammy Jane Hillyer, really
runs the division while he works jigsaw
puzzles. She's our people. We like her.

DENISE
Jigsaw puzzles? Wow.

***

"Let's go ahead and convene," Dr. Grim said as the faculty quieted their chatter. "We have the privilege today to have our sessions facilitated by two of College Retention and Persistence's most capable consultants, Gordon Chin and Marcus Richfield. Mister Chin is going to guide us through the first workshop, which is geared toward crystallizing our institutional identity. Please welcome Mister Chin.

[Incredibly weak applause. Sad really.]

"Oh, thank you, Clary-Smith all-stars," Chin began. "Wow, this is a championship-caliber faculty. As Doctor Grim explained, today we are going to put our collective effort into brainstorming the elements of our institutional identity that weave the fabric of this fine university. We will do that by identifying the specific elements of our institutional identity and then pairing them with our feelings about those elements. You will see two stacks of sticky notes on your tables that will help you through this next hour-long activity. The blue sticky notes will be used to fill in the blank in this statement: 'Clary-Smith's institutional identity is built upon blank.' Your orange sticky notes are for your feeling words. How do you feel about the words you have written on the blue sticky notes? So for example, if you write on a blue paper 'Clary-Smith's institutional identity is built upon tradition,' you would write on the orange paper that it makes you feel proud."

"That's it," Georgiana announced with defiance. "I'm out. Going to my office to write my world lit II syllabus."

"The duchess of eternal grudges has spoken. Let no man try to stop her," Meryl announced regally.

"Clary-Smith's institutional identity is built upon gross financial mismanagement, and that makes me feel grumpy," Livie offered.

"Clary-Smith's institutional identity is built upon reactive decision-making, and that makes me feel scared for my job," Roger added.

"Clary-Smith's institutional identity is built upon administrative incompetence, and that makes me feel exasperated," Meryl said.

"Clary-Smith's institutional identity is built upon sports, and that makes me feel like gouging out my left eyeball with a shrimp fork," Roger concluded.

"We know lots of words," Livie giggled. "I think the consultants underestimated how long this could take."

"Guys, I can already tell this is going to be pointless," Meryl said, standing up. "I am stepping over to my office for a few minutes to meet with Savannah Walters. Financial aid has put a hold on her account because her family is having trouble paying for her tuition. She won't be able to register for classes if someone doesn't help her. Cover for me if Huckleberry Grim asks."

"You got it," Roger said.

***

"Hello, partial English faculty," said Ronald Grim as he approached their sticky-note covered table with a plate full of stale bagels. "I haven't seen Doctor Kaiser or Doctor Ponsonby in this session. Remember these professional development opportunities are mandatory, Doctor Green. You should insist that your faculty participate."

"Doctor Ponsonby has been in the bathroom with catastrophic diarrhea for the last hour," said Livie, trying not to crack a smile. "The cafeteria's bagels strike again. Doctor Kaiser is in her office, meeting with a student who may not be able to return to the university unless somebody helps her figure out a solution for her financial hold. She will be back soon."

"It's Doctor Kaiser's job to attend required workshops," Grim said. "That's what she needs to be focused on. Tell Doctor Ponsonby that she has to return for the afternoon session or schedule a visit with the school nurse. She can send her appointment verification paperwork to Tammy Jane."

"Where, might I ask, are the business faculty?" Livie asked. "They never attend these things. Maybe that's because they all play golf with the president on Fridays instead of teaching classes, and he just lets it all slide. And Doctor Kaiser is well aware of what her job is: to attend to the needs of students and keep them here so our doors stay open. We can't even get a box of staples from the business office at this point. We clearly need the revenue."

"Doctor Green, what faculty in other divisions do is none of your concern. Why don't you work on making sure your faculty are in compliance with the university's professional development requirements?"

DENISE
Man, you think fast.

                                    ROGER
                And nice touch with the diarrhea.
                I would never have been able to
                    come up with such a solid
                (err...runny) excuse for Ponsonby
                so quickly and on the spot like that.

LIVIE
With a mouth-breather like Grim
for a supervisor, you have to keep
a few canned excuses at the ready.
The more they make him feel
uncomfortable for asking, the better.

ROGER

Our priorities are so off-kilter. I mean, how can you justify making a faculty member sit in a brainstorming workshop when a student has a legitimate need and faculty intervention might help the institution retain tens of thousands of dollars? They are so removed from the classroom that they have no idea what we do.

LIVIE

The deans don't get any credit for the conversation that keeps a student and her tuition revenue here. They get credit for 100% of their faculty attending a required workshop. That checks the box.

To: AllFaculty
FROM: Turnmire, Parker
SENT: Tue 8/11/10 2:01 p.m.

Colleagues,

For those of you teaching courses with research components this semester, please take a moment to chat with your students about ethical scholarly behavior and respect for shared academic materials. It came to the library's attention late last semester that dozens of circulating books have been defaced. It seems some students are ripping out the pages they need for their projects.

Parker Turnmire
Director of Library Acquisitions, Clary-Smith University

LIVIE
I'm in the most pointless meeting of my entire professional career, and I was just notified that students are ripping pages out of library books because they are too frigging lazy to take notes. I need my brother to make me laugh.

CARTER
Today I was driving out in the country to do a real-estate inspection. The delivery truck in front of me backfired, and I saw a whole field of fainting goats just lay out all at one time. I have never been happier in my whole life.

August 12, 2010

Clary-Smith Clarion
A Covert Faculty NEWSPAPER

Because higher education is a dumpster fire, and we don't have the budget to buy extinguishers

Head men's soccer coach Champ Rialto just returned from a month-long university-funded trip to Argentina, where he recruited for his soccer team. For the past three years, under his direction, the athletics program has overspent its allotted budget by nearly $4,000,000, and nobody has said boo, mainly because of Champ's willingness to provide regular, and apparently satisfactory, cunnilingus to Finance Director Karen Reynolds. Meanwhile in the English program, Dr. Livie Green was recently called in to the business office to reconcile receipts for a summer conference trip for which she received a cash advance. Because she tipped her dinner server 20% instead of the 15% allowed by business office policy, she was forced to pay back the $1.08 difference. Her only choice, of course, was to pay the business office with 108 pennies in a dirty sock. We'll let that 4 mil just fly away with the breeze for sports, but by God, we have to follow the letter of the law with gratuity.

In related financial news, the Clarion hears that the president's wife insisted that his renegotiated contract include a clause providing for twice-weekly maid service for the presidential mansion. In her defense, it's hard work sunning yourself in the backyard of the president's house right next to a busy sidewalk while wearing a bikini that should have rotated out of your wardrobe 20 years ago.

The General Education Committee managed to make it through the academic year 2009-2010 having accomplished absolutely nothing. This year promises to be equally ineffectual. Chairman Hannah Powell will rationalize waiting yet another year to begin the course-embedded assessments required by our accrediting body, the Southern Coalition of Rural and Metropolitan Private Institutions. According to Powell, the committee needs more time to "research best practices." Her administrative philosophy has always been that procrastination on her part will constitute an emergency on your part because she has been here longer than you.

The Dean of Nothingness finally completed the 1,000-piece jigsaw puzzle of the Hong Kong skyline Friday. It has occupied the majority of his office time since last week. "Boy it was a hard one," said Tammy Jane Hillyer, his administrative assistant. "The buildings in the cityscape were mostly in shades of taupe, and I thought he was going to have a come-apart on somebody before he could get that thing figured out."

In regards to Parker Turnmire's recent email about the defaced library books, everybody knows it was the lacrosse players. Dumbasses.

Finally, art professor Dutch Alder was forced by the administration to refund the $56 collected so far for the art program raffle because the Baptist Women's Alumni Association filed a complaint. Apparently, the Baptists view raffles as gambling, and the BWAA managed to bend the ear of a trustee about it. We can't have students losing their witness with raffle tickets. Crisis averted.

LIVIE
Well, it looks like I'm the lucky winner. The president's son gets to retake Introduction to College Writing with me. He just appeared on the roster of my 2:00 MWF section.

DENISE
Who is this?

MERYL
Tripp McLovelace, the president's demon spawn. I think he's a third-year freshman based on his current credits.

ROGER
He refuses to write papers or complete homework, so he has failed ENGL 101 three times now.

DENISE
I get that he's the president's son, but how is he still at the university if he fails classes?

GEORGIANA
If you pay, you stay. It's the Clary-Smith way. And besides, they need him on the lacrosse team. He's the captain.

DENISE
Sorry for so many (probably naive) questions, but aren't there athletic rules about minimum GPA requirements for student athletes?

GEORGIANA
There are rules for a lot of
things, but that doesn't mean our
Athletic Director gives a flying
fanny fart about any of them.

ROGER
Champ Rialto is a prick.

DENISE
And SCRAMPI. What is that again?

GEORGIANA
It's our accrediting body, but
I think it sounds more like a
venereal disease.

ROGER
"That hooker gave me scrampi."

MERYL
"She caught scrampi on spring
break in Daytona Beach and
needed antibiotics."

LIVIE
It makes me think of buttery shrimp
with a nice firm linguine.

To: AllStudents; AllFaculty; AllStaff
From: Admissions
Sent: Mon 8/16/10 12:04 p.m.

The Admissions office would like to celebrate all freshmen and returning students on the first day of classes. Please stop by the courtyard beside the Administration building today between 1:00 and 4:00 p.m. for some free popcorn and a romp in our double-decker bouncy house. Balloon artist Hager Jones will also be on hand making balloon squirrels as we welcome you all back to the nest!

ROGER
We have hired a man to make squirrels
out of balloons for the students.

LIVIE
You know, Admissions has always
refused interactions between prospective
students and faculty because they say
the students might find that to be boring
or intimidating, and we might scare them
away. Their excuse has always been
that the student development literature
suggests anything "academic" that happens
before the first day of classes could
deter a student from choosing a specific
university. This generation of students, the
experts say, is more interested in campus
amenities, extracurricular activities, sports
opportunities, and nightlife. Well, here we
are on the first day of academic classes, and
they have rented a double-decker bouncy
house and set it up on the front lawn.

GEORGIANA
I. NEED. STAPLES. How are these other
departments allowed to spend money right
now? And on the stupidest of stupid shit.

To: Green, Olivia
FROM: Caldwell, Trystyn
SENT: Tue 8/17/10 1:46 a.m.

doctor g so sorry I missed class yesterday I couldn't find our classroom where is Yarbrough 100

To: Caldwell, Trystyn
FROM: Green, Olivia
SENT: Tue 8/17/10 8:01 a.m.

Trystyn,

Yarbrough 100 is the same room where our freshman seminar class met last semester.

Dr. Olivia Green
Associate Professor of English, Clary-Smith University

To: Green, Olivia
FROM: Caldwell, Trystyn
SENT: Tue 8/17/10 10:55 a.m.

oh

To: Green, Olivia
From: Coughlin, Mitchell
Sent: Wed 8/18/10 8:49 a.m.

Ms. Green,

I am writing to inform you that the bill for Hickory Grove Printing, Inc. for $3,225 dated 4/6/10 to produce the campus literary magazine was not paid by the business office this summer. When you submitted the check request form in April, you signed the second page but did not initial your agreement to the terms on the first page. Therefore, the bill was not paid and is now in collections. You need to contact the vendor about this payable and let them know your error caused the delay.

Mitchell Coughlin
Accounts Payable Director, Clary-Smith University
Associate of Applied Science, '09

To: Coughlin, Mitchell
From: Green, Olivia
Sent: Wed 8/18/10 8:58 a.m.

Mitch,

Why didn't you email me in April to let me know I forgot to initial the form? Better yet, I was here in late June meeting with you to reconcile my conference attendance cash advance. Why didn't you say anything then? And is a missing initial on a form I did actually sign enough to hold up a check that puts the university into trouble with a debtor?

Dr. Olivia Green
Associate Professor of English, Clary-Smith University

To: Green, Olivia
FROM: Coughlin, Mitchell
SENT: Wed 8/18/10 9:07 a.m.

Ms. Green,

My name is Mitchell, not Mitch. It is the faculty member's responsibility to complete the business office's forms by following any and all instructions. Feel free to stop by my office today and initial the form. Once you do, I can begin the process of requesting a check.

Mitchell Coughlin
Accounts Payable Director, Clary-Smith University
Associate of Applied Science, '09

To: Coughlin, Mitchell
FROM: Green, Olivia
SENT: Wed 8/18/10 9:12 a.m.

Mitch,

My name is Dr. Green, not Ms. Green. I am having lunch with the Provost this afternoon, and I will make her aware of the situation. My guess is that she may have time to stop by in my place and check all the boxes on that form for me. The efficient delivery of the academic program is her top priority, after all.

Dr. Olivia Green
Associate Professor of English, Clary-Smith University

LIVIE
I just had another run-in
with Mitch the Bitch.

GEORGIANA
Oh God. You didn't call him
Mitch again did you?

LIVIE
Of course I did. I will
never call him "Mitchell."

GEORGIANA
Shit, Livie. Now he's going to hold up my check
request for the departmental field trip to the
Chapel Hill Press. I have to get it this week or
else I'll have to pay it myself and wait for a
reimbursement. That is literally the smallest
slice of power I have ever seen corrupt a
person. How does he still have a job?

To: Green, Olivia
From: Taylor, Gloria
Sent: Wed 8/18/10 11:15 a.m.

Dr. Green,

I don't have time for our lunch today to discuss your ideas for
the English program. Major textbook problem in the Dean of
Learning's office. Can I take a rain check?

Dr. Gloria Taylor
Provost, Clary-Smith University

To: Taylor, Gloria
From: Green, Olivia
Sent: Wed 8/18/10 11:21 a.m.

Dr. Taylor,

Absolutely. Another time. If you get a chance, please stop by and ask Mitchell Coughlin to show you the literary magazine printing bill that is now in collections because he refused for four months to tell me that I forgot to provide an initial on one of the forms, despite the fact that I was in his office face-to-face in June. We will never be able to use that vendor again because of these games. They cause damage to Clary-Smith's reputation in the community.

Dr. Olivia Green
Associate Professor of English, Clary-Smith University

To: Green, Olivia
From: Taylor, Gloria
Sent: Wed 8/18/10 11:25 a.m.

I will pay Mr. Coughlin a visit then. Thanks for understanding about lunch.

Dr. Gloria Taylor
Provost, Clary-Smith University

To: AllFaculty
From: Grim, Ronald
Sent: Wed 8/18/10 11:41 a.m.

Colleagues,

The Provost's office has just informed the deans that due to a regrettable error, Fall 2010 textbooks were not ordered for our students through the new textbook portal. Therefore, students should expect a significant delay. Because many common college textbooks are backordered at this time, it may be September 30 before all books are delivered. I recognize that current photocopy restrictions are going to pose a challenge to faculty trying to put materials on reserve in the library, as they will need to keep their own textbook copies instead of leaving them for students to access. One possible solution would be for faculty to avoid assigning any textbook readings until student books have arrived. Thank you for your willingness to help our students succeed in spite of this setback.

Dr. Ronald Grim
Dean of the Humanities and Sciences, Clary-Smith University

GEORGIANA
Sure thing, Ron. I'll tell students in my Jane Austen, British Literature, and World Literature courses to hit the pause button for A MONTH AND A HALF.

ROGER
How does the administration forget to order textbooks?

LIVIE
I think the Dean of Learning did it. The Provost had to cancel our lunch because of it.

MERYL
Seriously. His whole job is collecting and storing our syllabi, hosting a monthly workshop, and ordering textbooks. If you are a dean, you can completely forget a third of your job and cause a campus-wide disaster that is going to negatively affect the learning environment of more than 500 students, and there are absolutely no consequences. It's stunning.

LIVIE
Hey, let's meet after classes are over today to figure this out. Bring your syllabi and rosters. With the help of the librarians through interlibrary loans and by raiding our own bookshelves and hitting up the thrift store book sections, we might be able to piece together enough books to cover our students.

GEORGIANA
That is a brilliant idea.

DENISE
Remind me again why you aren't
our dean?

LIVIE
Because I can find my butt with both
hands. They don't want my kind
among their ranks.

ROGER
And what photocopy restrictions?

LIVIE
I truly do not know. That must
be coming next. It might be a
good idea to print your handouts
and assignments for the
whole semester now.

August 19, 2010

Clary-Smith Clarion

A Covert Faculty NEWSPAPER

Because higher education is a dumpster fire, and we don't have the budget to buy extinguishers

The lacrosse team crashed the Student Activity Board's "Safe Sex" Trivia game Saturday night. Student Veronica Sanchez-Arellano, who was in attendance, said, "It was legit like having Beavis and Butthead there. They answered every question with either 'chlamydia' or 'clitoris' and then giggled like pervs."

Aged Registrar Peter Hines continues to resist the digitization of the university's academic records, insisting instead that faculty "submit their grades in a vanilla folder." (He obviously is confusing "vanilla" and "manila.") His eyesight has deteriorated to such an extent that his attempted emails are almost unintelligible due to typos. Bless.

Sources with knowledge of the ding-a-lings in the business office advise all faculty and staff to avoid getting any personal money tangled up in university business, as reimbursements are averaging 120 days or more to process. Petty cash has also been unavailable since the beginning of the semester. It's just a shit sandwich over there. Don't get involved if you can avoid it.

Sources inside the Admissions department who insisted on retaining their anonymity say that projections for Fall 2011 enrollment are "BAD in all capital letters." Every year, we hope that the institution's financial distress will finally be sorted out. Don't hold your breath, friends.

Finally, Reverend Fitzgerald Duval reports that the $25,000 in unrestricted grant money that the Clary-Smith Baptist Church collected over the summer is mysteriously listed as "unavailable" on their budget report, and calls and emails to Finance Director Karen Reynolds have not been returned. The Clarion staff will continue to follow this story, as Reynolds is just as mean as menopause and deserves the heat. Her pattern of showing up at faculty meetings having conveniently forgotten to bring her spreadsheets in order to provide concrete answers to legitimate questions makes Duval's report even more intriguing. Stay tuned.

To: AllFaculty
From: Taylor, Gloria
Sent: Thur 8/19/10 9:17 a.m.

Esteemed colleagues,

Welcome back to another academic year full of potential at Clary-Smith University. I am delighted to be working with you in what is sure to be a critical year of improvement and advancement for the institution. We have some challenges to overcome, but we will do it together in true Clary-Smith fashion.

I wanted to take this opportunity to announce a very exciting program that will reduce the university's environmental footprint significantly: the Squirrels Go Green Initiative. Effective immediately, the university will transition as much as possible to a paperless organization. Every faculty member will be allowed to make 10 total photocopies each semester. Instead of printing, faculty will use the online learning platform to post documents that students may access. If you have any questions, please feel free to stop by my office for a chat. We will not put a governor on the copy machines at this time, but we do ask that you respect the limits.

Dr. Gloria Taylor
Provost, Clary-Smith University

GEORGIANA
... because we can't afford to add
governors to the copy machines.
Left out that part.

ROGER
Question: are we really "going green"
considering there are no recycling
receptacles anywhere on campus?

MERYL
So the majority of our students
don't have personal laptops. How
are they supposed to access the
online learning platform to see the
handouts in class?

LIVIE
Calm down, everybody. We need
to pause to make a word cloud.
That will pull us out of this tailspin.

To: AllFaculty; AllStaff
From: McLovelace, Grady
Sent: Thu 8/19/10 10:00 a.m.

The administration has become aware that a publication calling itself "The Clarion" has been appearing again several times a week under faculty office doors. The senior cabinet along with Human Resources is working to determine who the writers and distributors of this slanderous newsletter are. "The Clarion" is NOT an authorized university news outlet, and any information contained in it should be viewed with suspicion. Its reporting about program closures is not accurate. Anyone with information about the origins of this subversive publication should report it to Human Resources immediately. Your anonymity will be guaranteed.

Dr. Grady McLovelace
Clary-Smith University President

DENISE
So...what is the Clarion that everybody keeps talking about?

MERYL
Oh boy. Where to begin?

LIVIE
The Clary-Smith Clarion is an underground faculty newspaper that has been published here for the last 70 years or so. Nobody knows who writes the articles. Every few days, a new edition slides underneath the office doors of selected faculty members. The university archivist has a copy of every edition since the 1960s. The back issues are a complete riot, especially the ones from the 1970s.

MERYL
The editor gets quotes by playing the telephone game. When you are asked by someone to ask another person a question for the paper, you never know if that person is the editor or someone the editor asked. You just get the answer and pass it back to the person who asked you, and it always ends up in the paper. Whoever produces the paper is a total genius. I have no idea how he or she has managed to never get caught.

GEORGIANA
Once you have been here for a while and it becomes apparent that you're cool, you will probably start getting them under your door. Mine started about six months after I got here.

ROGER
There is a mole who immediately takes each new edition to the administration. They have tried to stop it for years. They even set up cameras in the hallways a few years ago to try to catch whoever was sliding the editions under office doors, but the footage never caught anybody.

LIVIE
We have a hunch that the editor rotates from year to year, but we aren't sure. The whole thing is hysterical, and the administration has no idea what to do about it, which is the glaze on the doughnut really.

To: Hillyer, Tammy Jane
From: Grim, Ronald
Sent: Thurs 8/19/10 2:02 p.m.

Tammy Jane,

I am getting ready to go home for the day, but I wanted to pass along a new working procedure that I think will help make our office more efficient. Today I spoke with IT about having all of my incoming telephone calls routed through your phone. The changeover should happen by the beginning of next week. I am just so busy, and answering phone calls is such a distraction.

When the call comes in, you will need to raise your voice and call the person on the other end of the line by name so I can hear who it is back in my office. I will then text you a thumbs up or a thumbs down so you will know if I am willing to take the call. If I give you the thumbs up, I want you to say "hold for Dean Grim" before you transfer the line. Your attention to this matter will help me tremendously.

Dr. Ronald Grim
Dean of the Humanities and Sciences, Clary-Smith University

[Forwarded Email]

Forward To: Green, Olivia
From: Hillyer, Tammy Jane
Sent: Thurs 8/19/10 2:04 p.m.

Livie,

I'm just going to sit here like a good Christian and not risk
my salvation by saying what is in my heart right now.

Tammy Jane

Tammy Jane,

I am getting ready to go home for the day, but I wanted
to pass along a new working procedure that I think will
help make our office more efficient. Today I spoke with
IT about having all of my incoming telephone calls routed
through your phone. The changeover should happen by the
beginning of next week. I am just so busy, and answering
phone calls is such a distraction.

When the call comes in, you will need to raise your voice
and call the person on the other end of the line by name so
I can hear who it is back in my office. I will then text you a
thumbs up or a thumbs down so you will know if I am willing
to take the call. If I give you the thumbs up, I want you to
say "hold for Dean Grim" before you transfer the line. Your
attention to this matter will help me tremendously.

Dr. Ronald Grim
Dean of the Humanities and Sciences, Clary-Smith University

LIVIE
I truly thought I had seen it all, but apparently this is the universe's way of saying "but wait...there's more." In my 3:00 freshman composition course today, I discovered that four of my students are Champ Rialto soccer recruits from Argentina who speak no English. I mean, they don't even know "Hello, my name is..." I asked them to take out a piece of paper and a pencil, and they just sat there with blank stares and didn't move. One of their teammates told me that they only speak Spanish, but he could translate anything important they needed to know, like assignments.

GEORGIANA
Same in my 2:00 section. I have two. I talked to Dutch Alder about it as we were coming out of class. He's on the Admissions Committee.

MERYL
Wait. We have a faculty Admissions Committee?

GEORGIANA
Yes, the committee reads all the applications and makes recommendations for who should be admitted and who should be denied. Then the Admissions staffers put that folder in a drawer and let everyone in. Dutch said that the administration was so concerned about enrollment in general and about the soccer team's lack of a divisional championship in particular that they temporarily suspended the minimum requirement for the English proficiency exam for non-native speakers.

ROGER
What?

MERYL
For the love of God. The Senate needs to know that right away.

LIVIE
I'm emailing Grim now. And I thought I was about to make it through the first week of classes without having to interface with him.

To: Grim, Ronald
From: Green, Olivia
Sent: Fri 8/20/10 11:09 a.m.

Dr. Grim,

It has come to the attention of several English faculty members today that numerous freshman soccer recruits from Argentina have gained entrance to the university without having a command of the English language. It appears that the mandate in the student handbook that requires a minimum score of 60 on the English proficiency exam was temporarily suspended for this incoming class. It will be impossible for these students to thrive in a writing class when they do not have access to the language of the professor, and it is unethical to knowingly enroll them in a class in which they have no chance to succeed. Please request assistance with this matter from the Provost as quickly as possible.

Dr. Olivia Green
Associate Professor of English, Clary-Smith University

To: Green, Olivia
From: Grim, Ronald
Sent: Fri 8/20/10 11:34 a.m.

Dr. Green,

Before you jump to conclusions about the academic capabilities of these students, I really must ask if you have done everything possible to meet them where they are.

Dr. Ronald Grim
Dean of Humanities and Sciences, Clary-Smith University

To: Grim, Ronald
FROM: Green, Olivia
SENT: Fri 8/20/10 11:39 a.m.

Dr. Grim,

Considering that I only had 50 minutes in our first class, which was devoted, as all first classes are, to going over the syllabus, I think I did a solid job of meeting them where they are, which, by the way, is at the corner of "Yo hablo Español" and "No hablo Inglés." I don't doubt the academic capabilities of these students. I do doubt their ability to speak, write, and comprehend English.

Dr. Olivia Green
Associate Professor of English, Clary-Smith University

To: Green, Olivia
FROM: Grim, Ronald
SENT: Fri 8/20/10 12:13 p.m.

Dr. Green,

That is not a very culturally sensitive approach to this issue. Can you verify which pedagogical strategies you employed to assist them? International students bring such wonderful diversity to our rural campus.

Dr. Ronald Grim
Dean of Humanities and Sciences, Clary-Smith University

To: Grim, Ronald
FROM: Green, Olivia
SENT: Fri 8/20/10 12:21 p.m.

Dr. Grim,

In my estimation, taking the tuition money of a monolingual student from Argentina in exchange for a year on the soccer field before he flunks out is the greater cultural insensitivity. Champ Rialto's recruiting method is carnivorous. I will take this issue to the Faculty Senate before the sun goes down if necessary.

Dr. Olivia J. Green
Associate Professor of English, Clary-Smith University

To: Green, Olivia
FROM: Grim, Ronald
SENT: Fri 8/20/10 12:25 p.m.

Dr. Green,

I will talk to the Provost and see if any easier classes are available for these students. Perhaps we can get them an English as a Second Language tutor to assist.

Dr. Ronald Grim
Dean of Humanities and Sciences, Clary-Smith University

ROGER
I just cleaned the keyboard in my office. It's the most responsible thing I've done in months. I felt like somebody should know.

LIVIE
Hahahahaha! You win the day. I just stole two reams of copier paper from the mail room when I saw that the office assistant stepped out to go to the bathroom. Our budget freeze has forced me to turn to thievery to get enough paper for classroom writing activities.

***

"Doctor Green! Welcome to the roof-top smoking lounge of the Edwin R. Nash Chapel." Reverend Fitzgerald Duval had a fat cigar already lighted and handed it to Livie as she flopped down into the rickety chaise lounge beside his.

"Preacher Fitz, this is a non-smoking campus with no tolerance or mercy for violators," Livie said as she exhaled the first glorious puff and smiled.

"We haven't had even a second to chat. How have the first few weeks of this academic semester treated you?" He accepted the return of the cigar as he and Livie laid back the heads of the chairs so the group of students passing on the sidewalk below couldn't see them.

"Well, half the soccer team can't speak English," Livie began. "One of my students from last semester can't find the very same classroom where we met for five months this past spring. My mama saw an hour-long news special about university shootings, and she keeps leaving non-teaching job applications on my porch like a stalker. Oh, and I haven't done my twenty jumping jacks today. That about covers it. What about you?"

Livie could already feel a little buzz from the cigar, and it made her thankful to have a friend with Cuban connections. The hot August sunshine on her face was just as delicious as the flavor of the smoke.

"Well, that sounds like business as usual on the academic side. I have been busy trying to appease the Baptist Women's Alumni Association. They are still all aflutter about Dutch Alder's scandalous raffle. You just don't get a group of bored and self-righteous Southern Baptist women riled up and expect them to settle down and play pretty afterward," Fitz said, stoking the cigar's fading ember.

"Well, somebody will die soon, and there will be casseroles for them to make and funeral services to critique. That'll divert their attention," Livie offered.

"My God, I hope so. I have a meeting with one of their committee chairs in fifteen minutes who is still just raging about it. She has a bad habit of getting out over her skis. It's just a matter of time before she face-plants."

"In that case, we need to keep this short," Livie said, standing up. "I've got to go lock horns with The Grimster over the placement of these soccer players. I would prefer the Baptist Women's Firing Squad over that."

"Be careful what you wish for, honey bun. I'll text you when I have a new cigar for you to try."

"You are truly the best pastor I know."

To: Green, Olivia
From: Caldwell, Trystyn
Sent: Mon 8/23/10 4:36 a.m.

dr g i cant complete my assignment somebody in my dorm STOLE my great Gatsby book i need an extension

To: Caldwell, Trystyn
From: Green, Olivia
Sent: Mon 8/23/10 8:11 a.m.

Trystyn,

The library has two copies of that book.

Dr. Olivia Green
Associate Professor of English, Clary-Smith University

SEPTEMBER

Clary-Smith

CRUCIFEROUS VEGETABLE CHALLENGE
SEPTEMBER 13-20, 2010

To: AllFaculty; AllStaff
FROM: Forsythe, Keesha
SENT: Wed 9/1/10 8:32 a.m.

Faculty and staff members,

I am excited to announce Clary-Smith's inaugural preventative health initiative, the first annual Cruciferous Vegetable Challenge.

Did you know that cruciferous vegetables are high in vitamin C and fiber and are a great source of antioxidants? Did you know that eating them daily can promote healthy weight loss?

The more cruciferous vegetables you eat, the better you will feel. Cousins in the cruciferous vegetable family include broccoli, cauliflower, brussels sprouts, kale, and bok choy.

The Cruciferous Vegetable Challenge will encourage all faculty and staff to eat at least two servings a day and document their meals in a food journal. The employee who eats the most cruciferous vegetables during the challenge week, which runs from September 13-20, will receive a $100 health savings account credit and be crowned the winner. Let's get fit together, Clary-Smith family!

To Good Health,
Keesha Forsythe, RN
Clary-Smith School Nurse

DENISE
I'm allergic to kale, broccoli, and bok choy. Am I required to compete in the challenge?

LIVIE
I think I'm safe in assuming that the Dean of Nothingness has already required Tammy Jane to create a Cruciferous Vegetable Challenge Exemption Form for faculty members who can provide medical proof to document their allergies.

GEORGIANA
No university mandate will compel me to eat healthy foods against my will.

ROGER
Hold on to your hats. I'm going to be the Cauliflower King! I need that $100 to pay for a dental filling I've been putting off. Game on.

MERYL
Broccoli freaks me out. It's those little
balls on the top. I just can't do it.

GEORGIANA
Employer intervention in my personal
life freaks me out. I don't want my inbox
filled with instructions for my private life.

DENISE
Don't you want Roger to get
his cavity filled, Dr. Kaiser?

GEORGIANA
We all know why he got that
cavity. It's that wretched
sugar-on-steroids pop
he drinks. Diet pop would
never do such a thing.

ROGER
For the love of God, Ponsonby.
You just can't let it go.

GEORGIANA
I love you more than potato chips,
Roger Eumenides, but I detest your pop.

ROGER

LIVIE
I feel the need to remind you all that
we are deep in the South here. "Soda"
and/or "sody" (if you are out in the country)
are the only acceptable alternatives. I don't
know what this "pop" foolishness is about.

***

The chapel rooftop was rainy and breezy, but that did not deter Reverend Fitz and Livie from huddling under a Southern Baptist Association umbrella to share the perfection of a Honduran cigar.

"So are you eating the vegetables?" Fitz asked, tapping the ash into a glass.

"That's going to be a really quick no from me," Livie said.

TAMMY JANE
Livie, The Grimster is extra punchy today. He
just asked me if I could try to pretend to be
more competent. You should poke at him to keep
things interesting.

LIVIE
I would be absolutely delighted.

Faculty General Assembly: Friday, September 9, 2010

PART IV: REPORTS FROM SELECTED DEANS
DEAN OF TEACHING
DEAN OF LEARNING
DEAN OF ASSESSMENT
DEAN OF ACCREDITATION
DEAN OF TECHNOLOGICAL INNOVATION
DEAN OF COMPLIANCE
DEAN OF COLLABORATION

"So here is the graph that shows test scores related to general education student learning outcomes from years 2005 through 2009," said Dr. Varner Earnhardt, Dean of Assessment, to the full faculty. "We began applying our assessments in year one (which was 2005 with a freshman class), and by the time those students reached year four (2009), their performance on the assessments was actually worse than it was in year one. Yes, Doctor Green?"

"That graph looks like an airplane headed straight into the ground," Livie said. "The decline in understanding of the learning objectives is unbelievable. Are you suggesting that our students actually knew less after spending four years here?"

"Well, the data from our assessments suggests that they performed better with the learning goals in their earlier years than they did in their later years," Dr. Earnhardt said, not even realizing the irony of the situation.

"I don't think a single faculty member in this room believes that our students not only did not learn from experiencing our general education classes but that they actually lost capabilities by participating in our courses.

Does data from course outcomes, as far as grades, demonstrate a similar decline?" Livie asked.

"Doctor Green, this is really not the place to get into specifics—" interjected Dr. Ronald Grim.

"Let her finish!" shouted Dutch Alder from the back row. "This is the precise forum for getting into specifics."

"This is the only place where deans are ever asked to be accountable to the faculty for their work," Livie continued. "Quite frankly, the Deans' Council filibusters. You make us sit through report after report at these general assemblies. You drone on to run out the clock so you won't have to face real questions at the end. Doctor Earnhardt, your data has to mean that your assessments were invalid. If you can't demonstrate a corresponding slide in student grades in these same courses, then your assessments are the problem. How else can you explain your doomsday graph there?"

"The answers you are asking for are really much more complex than I can explain with the limited time I have left," Earnhardt mumbled.

"Well, in that case, please let me use your remaining time to ask the faculty assembly a few questions," Livie said, gathering steam while also trying to prevent that same steam from shooting out of her ears.

MERYL
Oh my word, Dr. Green is about to do a thing.

ROGER
Look at the nerve on that girl.

GEORGIANA
Preach.

"We just heard about a very expensive four-year program that yielded negative results," Livie explained. "What would happen to teaching faculty members if 100 percent of our students failed our classes? The General Education Committee did nothing last year. And I mean literally nothing. Read their minutes. Now their four-year assessment program reveals that absolutely nothing was accomplished there either. We have deans for teaching and deans for learning. I still need somebody to explain why we need two separate positions for that. Faculty are the ones under the microscope. The administration is assessing the absolute doodle out of us, and yet they are never themselves assessed—and they buck us when we dare to ask even the most basic questions."

GEORGIANA
Standing Ovation. STANDING OVATION!

DENISE
So, are we storming the president's
mansion after this or what?

LIVIE

Do you ever just get the urge to do something totally reckless and irresponsible? At work today I planned out a scenario that would have me riding around hitting random mailboxes with a baseball bat. I don't even have a baseball bat. You were my driver. Isn't that what brothers are for?

CARTER

Of course. And I don't just think about it. I'm a firm believer that you have to act on it every now and then just to remind yourself that you're still alive. Just the other night, I shot out a street light in my apartment complex with a BB gun and then ran through the woods to see if I could elude capture. I felt like a 10-year-old hellraiser again.

LIVIE

Well your tax dollars paid for that light pole to be there in the first place.

CARTER

Damn straight. Do it, Dr. Dumbass. Hit somebody's mailbox with a baseball bat. I'll drive you, supply the bat, and pay you $20. You didn't do near enough shit as a kid. You need to catch up. It's good to see that you are now regretting your stalwart refusal of my bad influence over your life.

LIVIE

I just feel so upstanding and responsible. It's exhausting.

CARTER

Some misdemeanor destruction of property will clear that right up.

To: Green, Olivia
From: Caldwell, Trystyn
Sent: Mon 9/12/10 10:45 a.m.

doctor g I am on the track team our bus leaves for a meet in 15 minutes i will not be in your class am I missing anything important

To: Caldwell, Trystyn
From: Green, Olivia
Sent: Mon 9/12/10 10:49 a.m.

Trystyn,

Anytime you are absent from a college class, you are missing something important. Remember the syllabus lists what we will be covering and what assignment is due in our next class meeting. It is always best if you can notify your professors well in advance of an absence. That way we can help you plan how you will keep up with the course content while you are away.

Dr. Olivia Green
Associate Professor of English, Clary-Smith University

September 12, 2010

Clary-Smith Clarion
A Covert Faculty NEWSPAPER

Because higher education is a dumpster fire, and we don't have the budget to buy extinguishers

News out of the art program is disturbing indeed. The business faculty, who for years have had their eye on Dr. Dutch Alder's art studios and gallery, finally succeeded in convincing the president (on the golf course on a Friday, no doubt) to give them what they want. Alder has been notified that he has to have all of his program materials removed from the Rice building by October 10 to make way for the university's new "Center for Entrepreneurship and Microfinance." In the open gallery space, business faculty are installing an aggressively large conference room table that will make them feel even more in control of Clary-Smith's trajectory. The upstairs gallery spaces will be converted into spacious offices that are more befitting of the kings of the universe. Of course, the Clarion will keep you posted about Alder's efforts to secure the basic necessities for his program.

When Clary-Smith University integrated its first African American students in 1964, several local families began protesting by driving through campus with oversized Confederate battle flags waving from the back of their trucks. The tradition has continued to this day, with future generations of the same local families protesting the cause using their own pickups and a variety of bigoted bumper stickers and signs with hand-painted hate speech. Folks around here have always used the colloquial phrase "Oh she's her Mama's stupid gone to seed" to describe people who fell out of the moron tree and hit every branch on the way down. The next time you hear the truck horn that plays "Dixie" tooting its way through campus, step outside to see a real-world application of that colloquialism.

The university's much ballyhooed new electronic sign was installed last week, and a ribbon cutting ceremony was held to unveil the project, even though nobody was quite sure why a ribbon was being cut for a sign. In any event, the sign was installed so close to the road that it blocked the view of drivers trying to make a left onto Highway 415 from the north side of campus. Two collisions (thankfully without injury) occurred within the first three hours after the ceremony. The next day, the installation crew was called back to campus to move the sign, except this time they moved it so far back on the lawn that passing motorists can't see it. Clary-Smith is now the proud owner of an $18,000 sign that is only visible to people walking on our campus. There was a middle ground there, but our administration wasn't wily enough to find it.

In case you needed a reminder, Dr. Varner Earnhardt, Clary-Smith's Dean of Assessment, makes $115,000 annually.

GEORGIANA
So a female golfer hobbled into my 9:00
Jane Austen class on crutches with ice packs
rubber-banded to both knees. How is it
possible to hurt oneself so severely so early
in the morning—at golf?

ROGER
Our golf coach makes them run suicide
sprints at 5 a.m. three mornings a week.

[Long pause]

DENISE
I just looked it up. Suicide sprints require
sporty people to run as fast as possible
between two lines in an effort to improve
their athletic prowess whilst trying not to die.

GEORGIANA
Holy hell. And for golf.

ROGER
Oh, Dr. Ponsonby, it's not just for golf. They
are learning teamwork and leadership. These
are marketable skills.

GEORGIANA
And sadism.

MERYL
So I'm reading this biography of a
polygamous church leader and seeing many
parallels between fundamentalist cults and
college sports.

LIVIE
A few weeks ago, one of my
students got a concussion
so severe that it altered her
handwriting. She lost the ability to
spell for a few weeks.

DENISE
Which sport?

LIVIE
She got whacked in the head with
some kind of athletic stick. That's
all I know.

GEORGIANA
Lacrosse? Croquet?

LIVIE
We don't have a croquet team. Yet.

GEORGIANA
If we did, the university would fly them
all to Houston for the Division III croquet
championships and ask us to reschedule their
final exams for the summer when we're not
getting paid.

To: Green, Olivia
From: Couch, Gabrielle
Sent: Mon 9/13/10 8:34 a.m.

Dr. Green,

I just had to tell you. Brett Ashley and Jake Barnes from "The Sun Also Rises" were the answers to the final question last night at my weekly trivia group. I got it right because of your Hemingway seminar, and my team won! It was so exciting.

Sincerely,
Gabby Couch

LIVIE
Is Todd McCallister getting married today?

CARTER
Not exactly sure.

LIVIE
What do you mean? You're in the
wedding, right?

CARTER
Supposed to be. Last night was the
bachelor party. When he passed out drunk
around 2 a.m., we dropped him off in the
middle of that corn maze off Highway 34
and took his pants and his phone.

LIVIE
CARTER. Oh my God. What if he doesn't
show up for his wedding?

CARTER
Hahahahaha! He was only a few
miles away from his house. He'll
find his way back. And it's his
second wedding, so it's not that
big of a deal. His fiancé Misty also
has man hands and a terrible
personality. If he dodges the altar
today, not only will he be saving
himself the inevitable alimony, but
we won't all have to wear tuxedos.

LIVIE
You should all be ashamed of yourselves.
Ride out there and check on him right
now. He could have choked on his own
vomit or something.

CARTER
Todd McCallister has been
blacked out in many a field in
his day. He knows better than
to choke on his own vomit.

To: AllFaculty; AllStaff
From: McLovelace, Grady
Sent: Mon 9/13/10 10:46 a.m.

From the Office of the President:

The Clary-Smith University administration is sad to report that after 42 years of operation, the dance and drama programs are being eliminated. The decision was made by the Board of Trustees at its June meeting. Clary-Smith is committed to the liberal arts educational model, and senior officials will find ways to bring the arts of dance and drama to students through alternative special programs that are under consideration now. These two programs will not be "taught out" over the next four years, so advisers in these programs should notify their majors that they need to change majors by December 1, 2010.

Yours in Service,
Grady McLovelace
President, Clary-Smith University

September 15, 2010

Clary-Smith Clarion
A Covert Faculty NEWSPAPER

Because higher education is a dumpster fire, and we don't have the budget to buy extinguishers

Dance and drama are dead at Clary-Smith, which is cool because the humanities are totally overrated anyway. What the university really needed was the three-week "engaged learning" field trip to Europe the administration just approved for thirty business majors and six faculty. Dance and drama students who are not interested in selling out their dreams for an alternative career need to change their university by January 2011.

The Dean of Nothingness has been snooping around the English program's data after learning that they have been voluntarily keeping a detailed database of program outcomes student-by-student for the last six years. Their data stream allows them to see how students perform through both qualitative and quantitative means from the first-year writing program through General Education literature courses to writing-intensive classes. The dean's interest is really like that first crotch itch that lets you know a raging yeast infection is coming. No good can come of this.

In the midst of Clary-Smith's financial crisis, the cross-country team has just received their shipment of new monogrammed track suits. At a cost of $185 each, these jacket and tear-away jogging pants combos are the most expensive uniforms of any team on campus, which is funny because during the entirety of the 2009-2010 season, the cross-country team drew a total of four spectators to its home events, and that included counting the assistant coach's mom twice for attending two meets.

After months in committee task force negotiations, the Alumni Board finally decided on knockout roses as the species to plant in the president's garden for its annual Landscaping Day. Several distinguished alums spent last Saturday planting the new bushes with the greatest care. Harvey McLovelace, the president's awful beagle, pissed on them all, and they were all dead by Tuesday.

To: Green, Olivia
FROM: Grim, Ronald
SENT: Mon 9/20/10 11:29 a.m.

Dr. Green,

I have read the five individual goals you submitted for academic year 2010-2011, and I am requesting that you revise goal two (Complete the manuscript of a novel). This goal is not really achievable considering your course load, and this idea of creative writing does not directly align with any of the institutional goals from the university's strategic plan.

Dr. Ronald Grim
Dean of Humanities and Sciences, Clary-Smith University

To: Grim, Ronald
FROM: Green, Olivia
SENT: Mon 9/20/10 11:41 a.m.

Dr. Grim,

Perhaps I misunderstood the assignment. I thought I was required to set individual goals for myself that would help focus energy on achieving my personal best this year. It would seem that one's personal goals shouldn't be critiqued and revised by another person. Furthermore, publishing a novel aligns directly with Institutional Goal 34 from p. 26 of the Clary-Smith Institutional Plan: "Clary-Smith's faculty will maintain the institution's exceptional tradition of scholarship by regularly publishing both academic and creative pieces and staying current in the research of their respective disciplines." As well, shying away from a goal that some may see as "unachievable" discourages ambition and motivation.

Dr. Olivia Green
Associate Professor of English, Clary-Smith University

To: Green, Olivia
From: Grim, Ronald
Sent: Mon 9/20/10 11:56 a.m.

Dr. Green,

The goal must be revised. If you do not produce this novel manuscript by the end of summer 2011, you will damage the Humanities and Sciences' percentage of individual goal completion. The Deans' Council set a "SMART goal" of 100% completion for the faculty. We need to "close the assessment loop."

Dr. Ronald Grim
Dean of Humanities and Sciences, Clary-Smith University

To: Grim, Ronald
FROM: Green, Olivia
SENT: Mon 9/20/10 12:03 p.m.

Dr. Grim,

You are manipulating faculty goals, which have to be based on institutional goals, to set your own goals? Let me guess, you all just read Dr. Bill Corning's article about Russian Doll SMART goals in The Journal of Higher Ed Today. Am I right?

Dr. Olivia Green
Associate Professor of English, Clary-Smith University

To: Green, Olivia
FROM: Grim, Ronald
SENT: Mon 9/20/10 12:13 p.m.

Dr. Green,

What we read is none of your business. Revise the goal.

Dr. Ronald Grim
Dean of Humanities and Sciences, Clary-Smith University

To: Grim, Ronald
FROM: Green, Olivia
SENT: Mon 9/20/10 12:14 p.m.

Dr. Grim,

I will not revise my ambition—or the goal.

Dr. Olivia Green
Associate Professor of English, Clary-Smith University

DUTCH
Since I'm the only person in the art program,
I don't have anyone else to share student
triumphs with. I wanted to let you know that
Daunte Cartrette got accepted to show his
work at the Fearrington Folk Art Show. It's a
very prestigious honor for an undergraduate
student.

LIVIE
Woohoo! Another Clary-Smith
Squirrel moving on up!

ROGER
Rad.

MERYL
Dutch, you do such a great job
of helping your students with
professionalization. You deserve
some applause too.

GEORGIANA
Right on!

DENISE
I have Daunte in my Postcolonial lit
class. He's an incredible student.

To: Green, Olivia
From: Caldwell, Trystyn
Sent: Wed 9/22/10 10:45 a.m.

doc g

i cant come to class today i drove over some glass in the road and i am worried my tire might go flat

To: Caldwell, Trystyn
From: Green, Olivia
Sent: Wed 9/22/10 10:50 a.m.

Trystyn,

You are a residential student, not a commuter. You should power through your worry and walk to class.

Dr. Olivia Green
Associate Professor of English, Clary-Smith University

ROGER

Guys, did you know that McJuicington comes
into the office early in the morning and blasts
Bob Dylan protest songs? I was minding my
own damn business and trying to grade papers
today when "Hurricane" was suddenly blaring
at 6:30 a.m. And I mean blaring.

GEORGIANA

Yeah, he started that several
months ago when the soda vendor
stopped stocking his grape soda in
the machine downstairs.

MERYL

Roger, the same thing happened to me a few
weeks ago, except it was "The Times They
Are a-Changin'." Scared the crap out of me.
Complete silence and then HARMONICA.
How can he even make it that loud with that
1970s stereo?

ROGER

And it is so creepy because it sounds
folksy and innocuous, but he is clearly
unstable. That old bastard is going to
snap. And I don't want him to chop
me up in little pieces while "Maggie's
Farm" drowns out my screams.

LIVIE

A few years before you guys got here, the
Dean of Nothingness decided that faculty
within the division should observe each other
and write teaching evaluations. The Juice
came to my American literature class and
wrote the most horrifically mean-spirited
observation you can imagine. It was just
devastating as a new faculty member. When
I asked him which one of his classes he
would like me to observe, he said "No" and
walked away.

GEORGIANA
This place is going to hell on scholarship.

DENISE
Livie, how have you survived here for so
many years?

LIVIE
The honest answer is that I shotgun
sleeves of crackers in my office
when it gets to be too much.

***

"Doctor Green, do you have a minute?"

"Of course, Jacob," Livie said. "This is my office-hour time. Come in and have a seat."

"Well, you had us read that 'Red Wheelbarrow' poem by William Carlos Williams for homework. I've been thinking about it ever since I read it, and I wanted to talk to you about it before class this afternoon."

"I'm delighted to hear that you read the homework carefully. I would love to know what you think about it."

"Well, I'm an accounting major, so I don't really know nothing about poetry. I'm probably way off. I've been confused by most of the things you have made us read this semester. But I grew up on a farm with my grandparents, and this poem just made sense to me."

"How so?"

"Well, the writer says in the opening lines that 'so much depends upon a red wheel barrow.' He then talks about the rain. That got me to thinking about rain on a farm. To some people it might be kind of silly to say that everything depends on a wheelbarrow that has been rained on, but when you work a farm, everything really does depend on the rain. Without it, you can't grow crops. And we sell the crops we grow and feed them to the livestock. Then if there is too much rain, it floods your crops, and you can't really work, so you lose a day. That balance between needing the rain but being frustrated by the rain is real to farmers. I think that is what William Carlos Williams is trying to say. But I don't know."

"Jacob, what you have honed in on is the very complex concept of balance that so many Modernist writers like Robert Frost and Marianne Moore were playing around with. You have applied that to a text that resonates with you, which shows really deep critical thinking skills. Your explanation is magnificent."

"I didn't know poetry could be about farms. Most people think people on farms are dumb," Jacob added.

"Poetry can be about anything, and I think the best poetry challenges these notions about what the subject of art should be. Who's to say a Shakespearean sonnet is any more important than Williams's poem about a wheelbarrow? I am really proud of your work. There is an awful lot that is wrong with our educational system right now. But students like you, Jacob, are the whole reason I teach. Please feel free to come to my office anytime to discuss what you have read. You are really perceptive, and you should have confidence in your ability to analyze literary texts."

"I appreciate that. I think you are a real good teacher, Doctor Green."

September 23, 2010

Clary-Smith Clarion
A Covert Faculty NEWSPAPER

Because higher education is a dumpster fire, and we don't have the budget to buy extinguishers

Did you know that cruciferous vegetables can cause severe gastric distress when consumed in large quantities, especially in people who are unaccustomed to eating them? Did you know that vegetables like broccoli can cause unimaginable gas that just slips out with no warning? Did you know that crucifers like cauliflower can trigger rapid uncontrolled bowel movements large enough to clog up industrial-grade septic systems? Did you know that the symptoms of cruciferous vegetable overconsumption can be so severe as to cause dehydration, disorientation, and missed days at work? Clary-Smith University's school nurse clearly didn't know these things either when she launched the 2010 Cruciferous Vegetable Challenge. I mean damn.

GEORGIANA
Clary-Smith's institutional identity is built upon CRUCIFEROUS VEGETABLES, and that makes me feel FLATULENT.

LIVIE
Hahahahaha! Hahahahaha!

ROGER
Well played, Ponsonby.

September 28, 2010

Clary-Smith Clarion
A Covert Faculty NEWSPAPER

Because higher education is a dumpster fire, and we don't have the budget to buy extinguishers

At its late August meeting, Clary-Smith University's Board of Trustees approved its 2010-2011 operating budget. Soon after, it was noticed that budget officers forgot to include the library—the whole thing—in its projections. When the error was discovered, the Clarion reached out to the Head of Acquisitions, Parker Turnmire, for comment. "Considering our annual budget allotment for the past five years," Turnmire explained, "it's no biggie. Truly."

English Professor Livie Green kicked ass and took names on the Faculty Assembly floor last Friday as she contested the report delivered by the Dean of Teaching, Dr. Olsen Ferrier, that indicated the passing rates of students enrolled in freshman courses were high enough that the university could significantly increase the class size for all introductory courses on the spring schedule. Green came to the meeting armed with the English program's own qualitative and quantitative data, which demonstrated a 40% failure rate in ENGL101 and a 35% failure rate in ENGL102 last spring. Ferrier was not at all prepared to answer a data-supported challenge to his plan. It is abundantly clear that increased class sizes will provide our underprepared students with even less access to remedial instruction outside of class times. The Clarion staff is with Livie and common sense on this one.

The free pens at the launch of the new Career Center were a huge hit. I mean it truly does not take much to thrill us at this point. Faculty are also excited about students actually having some help with resumes, interview preparation, and job searches now.

Finally, a heads up. Don't even ask website manager Colton Randolph about his gluten sensitivity. Just trust us on that.

***

"So I heard you spoke a little truth to power the other day in the assembly, Doctor G," said Fitz, twisting the end of the shaggy beard Livie had been trying to convince him to shave for more than a year. "You do know you are Deans' Council Public Enemy Number One now, right?" The Nash Chapel Rooftop Cigar Bar was featuring delightfully sweet cigarillos on what was a gloriously sunny Thursday.

"I did indeed, pastor. And their attempt at intimidation was swift," Livie explained. "That afternoon Doctor Rickles, the Retention Czar, cornered me in the hallway to talk about the beautiful fall foliage on campus. But I knew what was coming—and it did."

"It's hard for me to wrap my head around how skinny Rickles is in comparison to his giant belly," Fitz said.

"He looks like a soda straw with a bad hernia. So there I stood with him in the hallway, and he said, 'You know, I had a long talk with your dean about what you said in the faculty meeting. He was not happy. That was a bold choice of words for a faculty member in such a low-enrolled program. Humanities departments are just dropping right and left around here. I'm surprised you weren't more careful considering this uncertain climate.'"

"Wowza," Fitz exclaimed. "So he didn't even try to protect himself from a bullying claim. Just put it right out there. This administration is building a house of cards. Something fishy is going on—at least with our finances. Karen Reynolds is behind it, I think."

"You do know that she and Champ Rialto spend almost every morning in the back of an athletics van out by Troy Lake," Livie added.

"I'm the one who told you about it last year, remember? They have just gotten more careless about it."

"I've changed my mind," Livie said in disgust. "Let's not talk about it."

MERYL

The president's wife just left my office.

GEORGIANA

What in the name of Charlotte Brontë?

MERYL

She just started making homemade
candles and decided to mosey on over from
the mansion and pressure faculty into buying
them during office hours.

LIVIE

She just left my office—after interrupting
my meeting with a student. She stuck
a snot-green candle under my nose and
called it "Woodland Frolic." I promise
that it had pine-scented cleanser in it. It
smelled just like my Nana's bathroom.
I can't unsmell it. I think the aroma is
permanently lodged in my nostrils.

ROGER

Pine-scented cleanser is highly flammable.
Not a good choice for a candle ingredient.

MERYL

I was assaulted by "Cinnamon Sparkle."
It had red glitter in it and smelled like
Christmas crawled up in that jar and
died a very painful death.

ROGER

Glitter is also highly flammable.

GEORGIANA

This is so unethical. I could just vomit.

DENISE

She got me with "Harvest Moon Dust."

LIVIE

I bet you a bucket of chicken she got
that name from a "Before and After"
puzzle on Wheel of Fortune.

GEORGIANA

Roger, is moon dust flammable? You are our
resident fire marshal now, right?

ROGER

There can be explosive fire in space, but
since there is no atmosphere there, the
explosion would make no sound.

MERYL

The moon does not have an aroma to my
knowledge. What did it smell like, Denise?

DENISE

I didn't smell it. When she told
me they were $45 each, I spontaneously
laughed out loud and she left. I'm
probably getting fired now.

September 25, 2010

Clary-Smith Clarion
A Covert Faculty NEWSPAPER

Because higher education is a dumpster fire, and we don't have the budget to buy extinguishers

We hear from faculty all across campus that Becky McLovelace, the first lady of Clary-Smith, has started a new line of wildly overpriced "artisanal candles." Under the moniker of "Pretty Perfections," she is making the rounds in the academic buildings and putting undue pressure on underpaid and overworked faculty members to buy them.

Music Professor Beth Hollins, in fear for her job, purchased one to give her elderly mother for her birthday. Her advice: "Please don't buy one. The wicks shoot sparks like a trick birthday candle. At my last visit, my mom's assisted living facility insisted that we put it out and remove it from her apartment. The scents are also totally oppressive. It's like a migraine and a safety hazard all wrapped up in one package."

If Becky is looking for new product line ideas, the Clarion staff put together a few concepts for her to consider. For a winter fragrance line, she could use the theme of infidelity paired with the aroma of garden florals. Products could include the "Your Husband Is Nailing the Women's Golf Coach" candle with a sweet geranium scent, or the "Your Husband Is Nailing the Chair of the Alumni Board" candle with a sassy rose fragrance. A tropical hibiscus scent could be incorporated into the "Your Husband Is Nailing the Education Department's Administrative Assistant" candle. With as much extramarital sex as President McShitface is having on this campus, the possibilities are positively endless.

A complementary line could include a candle called "Midlife Disappointment," characterized by a soothing lavender, or the "Resentment and Unexpressed Rage" candle with a bold herbaceous blend of basil and oregano. Go get 'em, Becky. The sky's the limit with Pretty Perfections!

Clary-Smith Fall 2010 Freshman Convocation Ceremony

Byron O. Keith Gymnasium
Saturday, September 29, 2010
10:00 a.m.

Processional	Dr. Beth Hollins (piano)
Invocation	Rev. Fitzgerald Duval
Greetings from Alumni Board	Brett Havendish
Keynote Address	Dr. Bart Hartmann, Professor of Religion, Mount Leonia College
Benediction	Rev. Fitzgerald Duval
Recessional	Dr. Beth Hollins (piano)

ROGER

Holy crap. This is the longest prayer in the
history of the world. Is it just me, or are we
about to have an altar call here?

LIVIE

Last week in the Convocation planning
meeting, McShitface asked Rev. Duval
to keep the invocation "short and
unchurchy" because the keynote speaker
is a very well-known atheist, in addition
to being a religion professor. We are in
for a rousing address called "Why we
should still study the IDEA of God even
though he actually doesn't exist."

DENISE
Huh?

ROGER

Oh, that is perfectly appropriate for a
Baptist-affiliated university with one of
the most traditional student-led campus
churches in the country. What a way to
know your audience, Clary-Smith.

GEORGIANA
#RhetoricalTriangleBitches

MERYL

And it explains why Rev. Duval
carried his shepherd's crook and broke
out his biggest pectoral cross for
the ceremony. Looks like something
Flavor Flav would wear on Sunday.

DENISE
Hahahaha!

GEORGIANA

My question is who would put up with
the torture of getting a doctorate when
you don't even believe the foundations
of your discipline are accurate?

LIVIE
Hey, is anybody seated with a good angle to see the Grimlin? During the last Convocation, Tammy Jane packed him a juice box and a Sudoku book to keep him occupied. An hour and a half is a long time for the little fellow to focus.

MERYL
Don't mind me. I'm just over here sitting under Dr. Hamilton's flabby left leg flank. Why do all these male business professors insist on sitting with their legs wide open?

GEORGIANA
Wieners! They sit like that because it gives the appearance that their dicks are so big they just can't manage their girth while sitting like average men.

MERYL
Ew. Ew.

GEORGIANA
Almost any query about the business faculty can be answered with "Wieners." Why is there never any consequence for their actions and they always get what they want? Wieners! Why would the whole business department vote against that exceptional curricular proposal that the rest of the faculty approved? Wieners! Why do they always schedule their required accounting class in conflict with my feminist rhetoric class even though they know some of their majors really want to take my course? Wieners!

OCTOBER

In honor of Breast Cancer Awareness Month, the Clary-Smith Health Services Office would like to encourage you to take your health into your own hands with this three-step breast self-examination that is so easy you can do it right at your desk!

Step One Raise your arm and put it behind your head.

Step Two Using the other arm and beginning at the outer edge of each breast, roll your fingertips around the entire breast with firm pressure, noting anything that feels unusual.

Step Three Squeeze each nipple and observe for any discharge.

If you notice any abnormalities, contact your physician for a screening immediately. And don't forget your annual mammogram!

To Good Health,
Keesha Forsythe, RN
Clary-Smith School Nurse

GEORGIANA
Call me old-fashioned, but I don't think we
should be touching ourselves at work.

LIVIE
We would have to be topless at our
desks to do this, no? Trying not to
overthink it, but maybe I am.

MERYL
I'm going to come in early tomorrow morning
and check my bare breasts for lumps while
McJuicington blasts "A Hard Rain's A-Gonna Fall."

DENISE
We probably shouldn't laugh about
cancer screening. We're awful people.

LIVIE
This university shouldn't fill my work inbox
with ridiculous emails that have nothing to do
with the performance of my job.

ROGER
I just took the sexual harassment
quiz required by HR, and I learned
from it that this is a conversation I
should not participate in.

GEORGIANA
Oh Rog, you can't be surrounded by this
many boobs and avoid getting tangled up in
an inappropriate conversation about them.

October 4, 2010

Clary-Smith Clarion
A Covert Faculty NEWSPAPER

Because higher education is a dumpster fire, and we don't have the budget to buy extinguishers

The Clarion staff was sad to learn of the passing of English professor Dr. Roger Eumenides's beloved uncle Gus Eumenides in a car accident last Friday in St. Petersburg, Florida. Despite his overwhelming grief, Roger somehow remembered his required "Faculty Absence form," which was created this year by the Dean of Nothingness simply to torment his underlings with extra paperwork. Eumenides filled it out immediately, documenting the need to fly out Monday and return that same day, missing only office hours and no actual class meetings. In short order, Eumenides heard back from Grim, who rejected the request for time off citing that Eumenides had not filed the form at least two weeks in advance as was required. Dr. Livie Green pleaded with the dean to do the right thing and let Eumenides travel and serve as a pall bearer in the funeral service. The dean wouldn't do it, claiming that the provost had informed all deans that faculty were not allowed to take any "personal days" during the academic year because they have the summer off. (Dr. Green managed to hold her tongue and did not remind the dean that faculty are NOT PAID during the summer, so it isn't exactly vacation.) In any event, Dr. Green told Grim that Dr. Eumenides tried to get his uncle's car accident scheduled for July, but there were no appointments available. She also pointed out that an Education faculty member last month took a week-long Western Caribbean cruise to Cozumel and Belize right smack dab in the middle of the semester, and the Dean of Education liked her Facebook pictures all along the way. Though English faculty offered to allow Roger to go to the funeral while they opened his office and staged it to appear as though he were on campus that day, Eumenides declined and instead watched the service via webcam during his office hours. In summation, The Dean of Nothingness should just lick a ball sack.

According to his administrative assistant, President Shady McShitface has fielded a number of complaints about faculty members from students in recent weeks. One student requested that faculty not be allowed to work out in the fitness center because Criminal Justice professor Dr. Stan Thomas "always leaves behind an old man smell on the treadmill." Two separate students complained that Dr. Bob Stuckey's diesel Ford F-350 pickup is loud and wakes them up every day at 9:00 a.m. when he gets to campus. Another student was upset that "we like have to read every day in that poetry class." Similarly, Dr. Burris's writing-intensive geology class was criticized for requiring "too much writing." Other highlights include the fact that "Dr. Waters always wears black, and it's depressing" and that Dr. O'Brien "doesn't know how to maximize a window when he's trying to show a video clip in class."

The Clarion staff extends its most heartfelt condolences to the family of Roger Eumenides and to these traumatized Clary-Smith students whose struggle is so very real.

To: AllFaculty
FROM: Hines, Peter
SENT: Fri 10/8/10 8:00 a.m.

Facluty,,

Before you leve for fall break, be sure to submittt your midterm
grade forms in a vanilla envelope in my my office no later than

5:0 today Friday

Peter Hines
Clary-Smith Registrar

DENISE
Bless his heart. Can somebody please help
Peter Hines?

GEORGIANA
He needs to be helped into retirement.

MERYL
We need the most detail-oriented person
we have in the role of Registrar. I can only
imagine the number of mistakes he makes in
student records.

LIVIE
A significant number of our graduating
seniors have to request new copies of
their diplomas because of typos. And
that paper is not cheap. Hines was just
not prepared for the digital age.

To: Green, Olivia
From: Caldwell, Trystyn
Sent: Fri 10/8/10 10:35 a.m.

doctor green i can not come to class today my stomach hurts

To: Caldwell, Trystyn
From: Green, Olivia
Sent: Fri 10/8/10 10:37 a.m.

Trystyn,

Go see the school nurse.

Dr. Olivia Green
Associate Professor of English, Clary-Smith University

To: Green, Olivia
From: Caldwell, Trystyn
Sent: Fri 10/8/10 10:54 a.m.

well it does not hurt that bad i just need to rest i think

***

Livie knew the very cigar she was inhaling was cutting her life short by a day, but, she rationalized, so was every interaction she had with sophomore Trystyn Caldwell. She took the smoke in and held it there for good measure.

"I'm afraid I'm going to need the faculty's help," said Fitz, running his fingers through his beard to get the cigar ashes out. "I think the administration is considering removing the protection of the Monday 11:00 a.m. chapel hour."

"What possible reason could they have?" Livie asked, totally stunned.

"Because the 11:00 a.m. hour on Monday is sacred, that means no classes can take place on Monday, Wednesday, or Friday at that hour. Champ Rialto has been pushing back for a few years because athletics wants student-athletes to be able to get all of their classes 'over with' as soon as possible in the day so the rest of their time can be devoted to sports. Just keep your ear to the ground. Because that protection is listed in the catalog, it may require a faculty vote to change it."

"Oh, it absolutely will," Livie confirmed. "I will go ahead and talk to David Miller. He's the chair of the curriculum board. He will let me know if he hears of anything coming around the corner. Hey, if I do this for you, will you shave your beard? Your face is just too pretty to be covered up."

"Here," Fitz said. "Put this cigar in your mouth and hush up."

October 8, 2010

Clary-Smith Clarion
A Covert Faculty NEWSPAPER

Because higher education is a dumpster fire, and we don't have the budget to buy extinguishers

All faculty recently received urgent emails from their deans requesting a list of their 2009-10 publications and conferences. The lemon in the tea was that not a single dean realized that information was already in their hands on the CVs that we update and submit annually.

It was recently announced that Ramona Pfizer has joined Clary-Smith as our new Admissions director. When asked for comment on the hire, Sociology professor Jim Culp made a sour face and said, "I don't trust anything or anyone with a silent 'p' in their name."

Frank Abbott, Clary-Smith's Facilities and Grounds Manager, was super mean to Communications professor Allison Barkley on Wednesday when it was discovered that she used inch-wide blue painter's tape to hang up flyers for the debate club interest meeting instead of the required half-inch-wide white painter's tape. The Clarion staff is reasonably sure Abbott hasn't been laid since the early part of the Reagan administration, so it's easy to see how painter's tape has come to occupy so much of his head space.

English professor Meryl Kaiser was totally puzzled yesterday as she drove her incredibly dirty minivan into campus, as random men in work trucks and tractor trailers kept honking their horns and waving. Once she arrived on campus and got her lunch bag out of the trunk, she realized her husband had used his finger to write "MY WIFE IS DIRTIER THAN THIS VAN" on the back.

The Sabbatical Committee has received 58 applications this year. There are exactly 66 faculty members on this campus. We are all apparently looking for a way out of this cluster.

To: AllFaculty
From: McLovelace, Grady
Sent: Sat 10/16/10 3:34 a.m.

Dr. Facelli,

My butthole itches a lot. I'm worried I have a hemoroid. Hemorroid. Hemmoroid. Did I spell that right? Hahaha haha. Hemmorhoid. I need an appointment with you soon. Please have your receptionist call my administrative assistant to schedule. My butthole itches a lot.

Grady

MERYL
So ... what are we looking at in our inboxes here? 3:34 a.m. from McShitface. Yikes on bikes.

LIVIE
OH MY GOD. I have been waiting to text you guys for an hour because I didn't want to wake you. He sent it to all faculty. This is unbelievable.

ROGER
What's happening?

MERYL
The president sent an email to all faculty at 3:30 this morning. There is no Dr. Facelli at Clary-Smith. That has to be his physician.

ROGER
Holy hell. I have never seen anything like it.

DENISE

Hahahaha. Hahahahaha. Hahahahaha.
Hahahahaha. Hahahahaha.

GEORGIANA

I just talked to Maddie Victor in the
Communications program. Her husband organized
a golf tournament fundraiser for the United Way
yesterday at the country club, and he says the
president was absolutely smashed when his team
finished up on the 18th green. He left an empty
bottle of bourbon upside down in the cup instead of
putting the pin stick back in. Then he went straight
to the clubhouse bar and drank enough whiskey to
kill most grown men. He blacked out near closing
time and pissed himself. The bartender ordered him
a cab home to prevent him from killing someone on
the highway.

October 17, 2010

Clary-Smith Clarion
A Covert Faculty NEWSPAPER

Because higher education is a dumpster fire, and we don't have the budget to buy extinguishers

BREAKING NEWS: McShitFace Reveals "Butthole Itch" in Email to All Faculty

Clary-Smith faculty were gifted Sunday morning with an unexpected email from President Grady McLovelace that twice disclosed that his "butthole itches a lot."

Once word of the email began to circulate, the Clarion was able to confirm from multiple sources that McLovelace was indeed drunk at the time the email was composed. He made a total ass of himself Saturday at the Hickory Grove Country Club's United Way Invitational.

The message, intended for Dr. Anton Facelli, the president's primary care physician, was misrouted by McLovelace in his inebriation, as he likely typed "Fac" for Facelli in his email directory, only to get "Fac" for Faculty instead.

No word yet on whether the Board of Trustees will finally take action and fire the son of a bitch.

The Clarion reached out to the head of the Nursing program, Dr. Robin Marshall, for clarification about what this symptom could mean. "What McLovelace was referencing is known as 'anal pruritus,'" Marshall explained. "It could be caused by a number of underlying conditions including hemorrhoids, or something as simple as poor bathroom hygiene." She recommends that he try a hemorrhoid ointment coupled with warm, moist compresses to the rectum and suggests that he wipe his bottom more thoroughly after bowel movements.

Since all four of McLovelace's attempts at spelling hemorrhoid were unsuccessful, we will post the correct spelling here for the record: hemorrhoid. Here it is in an example sentence: Grady McLovelace has hemorrhoids that make his butthole itch a lot, and the faculty couldn't be happier about it.

To: Green, Olivia
From: Caldwell, Trystyn
Sent: Mon 10/18/10 10:53 a.m.

doctor g i can not come to class today my dog's stomach hurts

To: Caldwell, Trystyn
From: Green, Olivia
Sent: Mon 10/18/10 10:55 a.m.

Trystyn,

Take your dog to the veterinarian.

Dr. Olivia Green
Associate Professor of English, Clary-Smith University

To: Green, Olivia
From: Caldwell, Trystyn
Sent: Mon 10/18/10 10:57 a.m.

i don't think it is that bad he just needs to rest

***

"Doctor Green, do you have a minute before you go to your next class?" Chris Shepherd held his literature anthology nervously as he thumbed to the appropriate page.

"I certainly do, Chris. What's up?" Livie put down her whiteboard eraser and leaned on the podium to listen.

"So I didn't want to say this in class because I was worried I was wrong," Chris started. "This 'Snow Man' poem by Wallace Stevens has me thinking. There's something to this 'mind of winter' part that he begins the poem with because he ends with a reference to nothing being there."

"You are definitely on to something. Here," Livie said, handing Chris the dry erase marker. "Draw the title. This poem is called 'The Snow Man.'"

Chris took the marker and drew a snowman complete with a carrot nose and top hat.

"Okay. Now point to that snow man in the poem," Livie instructed him.

He stood for a few minutes scanning the text and finally looked up. "He's not there. Nothing is there."

"Exactly," Livie said with a smile. "You were on the right track from the start. Stevens sets us up with the visual of a traditional snow man, but that is not what he delivers at all. Instead, the poem begins with a hypothetical person who has a 'mind of winter.' Remember what we said about modern writers: if it was hard work to write, they want it to be hard work to read. Wallace Stevens is having fun with you here. What is this poem about, Chris?"

"It's about what happens in the mind when the reader does not get what is expected," Chris said with confidence.

"Precisely. Wallace Stevens doesn't care about snow men. He cares what your brain has to do to sort through a poem that is set up this way. That activity of the mind is his jam. That is what he was after. Your brain was doing the work, and you didn't need my help for that to happen. I'm impressed. As we continue to read these modern poets, always keep in mind that they are pushing boundaries and experimenting in really incredible ways. That is what makes them challenging but fun. Well done, sir."

"Thanks, Doctor Green. This is really cool."

"It makes my day that you think it's cool."

October 21, 2010

Clary-Smith Clarion
A Covert Faculty NEWSPAPER

Because higher education is a dumpster fire, and we don't have the budget to buy extinguishers

The shit stain that is the chair of the business program, Dr. Toby Zink, has struck again, this time asking Writing Center director Livie Green if his faculty could use part of the Writing Center space to store some old filing cabinets because "you really don't need a whole room just to fix commas, right?"

Clary-Smith's longtime Institutional Research director, Dr. Gladys Myers, has been observed wearing her sweater vest inside out again, and her pattern of scheduling meetings in rooms that don't exist is ongoing.

History department superstar Dr. Scott Gardner was reprimanded last week for sending an email to the president announcing the publication of his forthcoming book with a top-tier academic press. Gardner was reminded of the chain of command: he emails the program coordinator, who emails the chair, who emails the dean, who emails the provost's admin, who emails the provost, who then emails the president—only if the item is deemed newsworthy. Get with the program, Scottie.

On Tuesday the Humanities and Sciences dean sent a pointed email to Mathematics program director Dr. Carrie Baker asking when data from the new First-Year Math program would be available. Baker had to remind the dean that the 40-page proposal she wrote advocating for the program was denied by the Deans' Council two years ago, and the program was never funded. The dean's response was "Oh. That's right. Never mind."

Finally, rumblings that the foreign language program may be in danger continue to find their way to Clarion staffers. We all know it's hard to learn Spanish from a professor with a lisp, but that is no reason to cut a program the students really enjoy. And Dr. Elena Crisp is just a super-nice human being. An informal Clarion poll revealed that 100% of the faculty would rather see literally any other dean fired than see the foreign language program close. Aside from her majors, Dr. Crisp's talents make it possible for students to take elective Spanish courses that actually make them more desirable on the job market. We recognize that applying logic to the decision-making process is a big no-no around here, though. So, whatevs.

October 25, 2010 Humanities and Sciences Meeting Minutes

NOTETAKER: GEORGIANA PONSONBY, DUCHESS OF ETERNAL GRUDGES
IN ATTENDANCE: 23 FACULTY MEMBERS
LATE BECAUSE HE IS A DAMNED MORON: DR. NOAH CAREY
IN ATTENDANCE BUT GRADING PAPERS: 16 FACULTY MEMBERS
PRESIDING: THE DEAN OF NOTHINGNESS

11:01 a.m.	The Dean of Nothingness fails to connect his laptop to the projector. Again. History faculty are asked to help because they are the youngest and the most likely to know where all the cords plug in.
11:05 a.m.	Connection achieved.
11:06 a.m.	Grown-ass adults with terminal degrees are castigated for saying a college class is "canceled" instead of saying "class has moved online today with an engaging alternative activity."
11:07 a.m.	Music Professor Dr. Michael Peach begins to sing an improvised song called "What in the Actual Hell?" to the tune of Beyonce's "Crazy In Love" under his breath. It is well received by his colleagues on the back row.
11:10 a.m.	The Dean of Nothingness has already referenced three ways in which the faculty are "out of compliance" with his requests. The stakes for posting office hour signs on our doors clearly have never been higher.
11:12 a.m.	The futility of the large group meeting becomes painfully apparent. Dr. Eumenides wonders to himself why academic leaders schedule meetings with content that could

easily be an email, but as a second-year faculty member, he is way too scared to say it out loud.

11:15 a.m. A second is required to bring the math curricular proposal to a vote, but everyone (including the math faculty) has zoned out. The Dean of Nothingness must call on a volunteer to move the motion forward.

11:17 a.m. Religion Professor Dr. James Aaron audibly gasps at the end of his yawn. Several faculty members chuckle. It's the most fun they will enjoy for the rest of the hour.

11:20 a.m. Professor Bob Harkey (Social Work) asks for a point of clarification in Robert's Rules because he knows good and well he's the only one in the room who has studied Robert's Rules.

11:23 a.m. Dr. Meryl Kaiser pretends to sneeze and then covers her nose as if she needs a tissue. She leaves the room to go listen to NPR in her car.

11:25 a.m. The Dean of Nothingness presents another slide containing outdated demographic data about majors. Professor Leo Putnam (Psychology) finds the correct data online in approximately 15 seconds, at which time it becomes abundantly clear that there is no reason for any of us to be here.

11:30 a.m. Dr. Olivia Green finally realizes what has been bugging her about the president's face. His protruding lower jaw makes him look like a grouper.

11:33 a.m. Dr. Allison Barkley (Communications) is fussed at for making a general announcement while the meeting agenda is currently on program announcements. Dr. Alder asks that the Dean of Nothingness explain the distinction again. He likes making him work.

11:34 a.m.   The biology faculty have used the last 34 minutes to write a new departmental attendance policy. It's good too.

11:37 a.m.   To give the illusion of cross-campus collaboration in his meetings, the Dean of Nothingness has invited the university's public relations director to field our questions about the new request process for press releases. We have no questions. We hate her. Her incompetence is stunning.

Sorry. I think I lost consciousness for a few minutes. Bet I missed some things.

11:53 a.m.   Dr. Alder makes a motion to adjourn because he has to teach across campus at 12:00. The Dean of Nothingness denies the request, saying "that's not for another 7 minutes."

11:56 a.m.   Faculty refuse to sign up for volunteer slots manning booths at the upcoming Admissions event for prospective students, citing the juvenile and frankly embarrassing activities offered at the same event last spring, activities which included a snow cone bar and pony rides. The Dean of Nothingness insists that recruitment is our responsibility. Nobody signs the volunteer form.

12:01 p.m.   Meeting adjourns. Dr. Alder is five minutes late for his class, sweaty from running, and livid that he will have to hold his peepee for the next hour.

MERYL
Outstanding minutes, Ponsonby.
The best ones yet.

DENISE
How do you get away with it?

GEORGIANA
The Grim Reaper never reads them,
and our accrediting body is never going
to come to campus and demand to see
them (as the administration always
threatens), so I decided that I might as
well have fun with them.

ROGER
Absolutely superb.

To: AllFaculty; AllStaff
FROM: McLovelace, Grady
SENT: Fri 10/29/10 4:59 p.m.

The Clary-Smith administration is sad to report that at the end of the Fall 2010 semester, the foreign language program will close. While it pains the Board of Trustees to lose another valued liberal arts program, there are so many new opportunities on the horizon for Clary-Smith's academic offerings. Because Clary-Smith is so dedicated to providing students with the education required to be global citizens, the administration is currently exploring the possibility of hiring an adjunct to teach one Spanish course per year.

Dr. Grady McLovelace
President, Clary-Smith University

October 30, 2010

Clary-Smith Clarion
A Covert Faculty NEWSPAPER

Because higher education is a dumpster fire, and we don't have the budget to buy extinguishers

The Education Department's annual Read-a-Thon lock-in Friday night was marred by poor institutional planning. The Student Activities Board haunted trail was scheduled for the same night and ended in the clearing of trees directly adjacent to the library. The second and third graders participating in the overnight literacy event could see the conclusion of the haunted trail through the library's very large atrium windows. Each time a headless ghoul chased a new group of screaming students out of the woods with a chainsaw, another traumatized child called home for an early pick-up.

Edgar Dewey continues to make disparaging jokes about red states on the faculty assembly floor. Ironically, he is the chair of the Diversity and Inclusivity Committee, and thus should really be on top of the whole tolerance thing.

The long-suffering Tammy Jane Hillyer finally received her lukewarm performance evaluation from Dr. Ronald Grim, despite the fact that she all but wipes his ass for him on a daily basis. When reached for comment, Tammy Jane had a dead look in her eyes that can only come from working for a man as horrible as Little Ronnie Grim. "At this point," she said, "if my vagina sprouted wings in the night and I woke up in the morning with it flying around me, I wouldn't be surprised."

Reverend Fitzgerald Duval is in hot water for his invocation at the last Faculty Assembly. He prayed that the administration would somehow figure out how to do their jobs so the university doesn't have to close. He also asked God to help the president to be less of a douche. The prayer got three "amens" and a "hallelujah" from the faculty.

Finally, two dozen students were caught skinny dipping in Troy Lake last weekend on an uncharacteristically cold October night of 29 degrees. Clary-Smith Police Officer Boyce Lowder, who couldn't crack a case if his very life depended on it, stumbled upon the orgy quite by chance in one of his nightly patrols. Apparently the communications center chatter was golden, with Lowder reportedly hollering, "I need backup! There's naked people running everywhere!" into his radio.

NOVEMBER

To: Green, Olivia
From: Caldwell, Trystyn
Sent: Mon 11/2/10 10:44 a.m.

doctor g i will not be in class today I hit myself in the face while opening a plastic fork and my lip won't stop bleeding

To: Caldwell, Trystyn
From: Green, Olivia
Sent: Mon 11/2/10 10:49 a.m.

Trystyn,

I don't believe there is anything I can do to help you there.

Dr. Olivia Green
Associate Professor of English, Clary-Smith University

LIVIE
You are the first person in my life who needed to know about this.

CARTER
Whatcha got?

LIVIE
One of my students actually admitted to hitting herself in the face while trying to open a plastic fork.

CARTER
It sounds like maybe the entrance standards for American colleges have declined.

LIVIE
You would be absolutely correct.

To: Green, Olivia
From: Hernandez, Carlos
Sent: Mon 11/2/10 2:12 p.m.

Dr. G,

I wanted to say thank you for helping me with my research paper over the weekend. Your guidance on my draft was so useful. I appreciate you working on a Saturday to help me.

Carlos

To: Hernandez, Carlos
From: Green, Olivia
Sent: Mon 11/2/10 3:56 p.m.

Carlos,

You are most welcome. I am impressed with your dedication to improving your writing.

Dr. Olivia Green
Associate Professor of English, Clary-Smith University

To: AllFaculty; AllStaff
From: Forsythe, Keesha
Sent: Tue 11/3/10 8:21 a.m.

Colleagues,

This month's healthy tip is about an aspect of your health that you might not think very much about: posture!

The proper carriage of your head and shoulders is critical to good muscular and spinal health.

Make sure you have a chair with good lumbar support. Be conscious of your posture, especially when you are working at your computer. Forward head posture and rounded shoulders while you work could contribute to headaches, muscle soreness, and less beneficial sleep. Sit up straight and improve your overall health!

To Good Health,
Keesha Forsythe, RN
Clary-Smith School Nurse

November 4, 2010

Clary-Smith Clarion
A Covert Faculty NEWSPAPER

Because higher education is a dumpster fire, and we don't have the budget to buy extinguishers

After being unceremoniously booted in September from his gallery space by the dickheads in the business program and never finding a suitable space in any other building that could accommodate his program, the ever creative and quick-thinking Dr. Dutch Alder has begun holding his studio classes out by Troy Lake under the historic Garringer Gazebo. Classes can meet rain or shine, and students can wash their hands and brushes in the lake. An added bonus is that Alder's students are truly inspired by the sights, smells, and sounds of the open space. As the weather turns colder, Alder will need an indoor location for class meetings, but for now, it feels good to see him win one.

The Clary-Smith community is now in the fourth month of Nurse Keesha Forsythe's enlightening preventative health program, which clogs up our email inboxes with messages that could not be any less relevant to our day-to-day jobs. This month's edition, which focuses on posture, encourages us to use "a chair with good lumbar support." The Clarion has learned from the budget report of the planned Lucas Rude Health Sciences building that the faculty and staff working there will all receive brand-new, ergonomically superior office chairs. Unfortunately, the faculty in the other buildings across campus will have to make do with the office chairs that have been in use since *The Fresh Prince of Bel-Air* made its television debut on NBC in 1990. And you guessed it—those chairs are not ergonomically superior.

Last week the Admissions office emailed a survey link asking faculty to provide feedback on the activities that were scheduled during Accepted New Squirrels Day. It went about as well as you would expect.

The cash advance for the 16th Annual Trunk or Treat event at the Clary-Smith Baptist Church that Reverend Fitzgerald Duval submitted back in July was never processed by Accounts Payable, thus Fitz had to front the Halloween candy money for approximately 650 children, or else there would have been nothing to hand out. Mitchell Coughlin is squarely to blame. Faculty and staff are used to showing up in hotel lobbies with the university credit card only to be told that it is maxed out, and they have to use their own card to have a place to sleep for the night. This, however, takes it to a new level.

The streak continues. Chemistry professor Bart Funk has made a motion to table every curricular proposal from the Exercise Science program since its inception in 1992. Funk continues to protest the legitimacy of the program, claiming, "you can't make a science out of exercising."

To: AllFaculty
From: Clary-Smith University Deans
Sent: Friday, November 5, 2010

At our October Policy Retreat in South Carolina, the deans discussed the issue of faculty comportment as it relates to professional attire. As a result, the Deans' Council voted unanimously to adopt a new policy and procedure designed to ensure all faculty are dressing appropriately and in a way that meets student and parent expectations.

Effective immediately, faculty will be allowed to wear "blue jean" style slacks only after receiving written approval from their program coordinator at least two weeks before the casual day is planned. Faculty members must use the attached Professional Attire Exception Request Form and submit it with the requisite signatures (along with the reason the exception is necessary) to their respective dean. All faculty without PAER forms on file on any given day are expected to wear business attire that complies with Clary-Smith's current faculty handbook policy.

The deans appreciate everything that full-time faculty do to preserve the classroom as a professional space.

MERYL
The entire starting lineup of the men's
baseball team showed up high to my
creative writing class this afternoon.
Like they give a shit what I'm wearing.
They were so blitzed they didn't know
what planet they were on.

GEORGIANA
Did you hear that the Deans' retreat was in
Charleston? They rented out the entire Wentworth
Mansion (21 rooms at $600 a night per room).
It was $25,000 total for the weekend just for
lodging. And they ate and drank like Henry the
Eighth at the very best restaurants in town.

DENISE
As this university falls
to its knees financially.

ROGER
And now we can't even choose our own
britches. That was their big "aha" moment
of the weekend. We should take away the
faculty's power to pick their pants.

LIVIE
The hell we can't choose. I'm the
program coordinator, and they pay me a
stipend of $1,000 a year before taxes to
have big ideas. Give me a few hours.

LIVIE

I'm making more photocopies at your
office this weekend. I'll leave reams of
paper to account for what I use.

CARTER

Sure thing. Tell me again why you can't
make photocopies where you work?
Seems to me that many PhD's could
figure out a way to pay to keep the
copiers running.

LIVIE

Oh, they can figure out solutions for the
programs they value. I, unfortunately,
chose the wrong major in college.

CARTER

Make as many copies as you need.
You know I don't mind.

LIVIE

Aside from that time when I was five and you
knocked the wind out of me when you were
pretending to be Ric Flair, you're the best
brother I could have hoped for.

CARTER

WOOOOOOO!

LIVIE

Also, I took Mama and Daddy to the Cracker
Barrel in Hickory Grove for lunch after church
this past weekend. Mama is reading her emails
out loud now–like the whole table (including
our waitress) needs to be involved. I think she
has sponsored a Nigerian child through some
kind of save the children charity. The next time
you're over there, ask to see the paperwork on
that to make sure it's not a scam.

CARTER

She's got pictures of that little boy all
over the refrigerator now because you
haven't given her any grandchildren yet.

To: Eumenides, Roger; Ponsonby, Georgiana;
Kaiser, Meryl; McGillicuddy, Denise
From: Green, Olivia
Sent: Fri 11/5/10 8:23 p.m.

Colleagues,

On Monday morning, you will find 75 pre-signed Professional
Attire Exception Request (PAER) forms in each of your mailboxes.
All you need to do is initial the bottom of each form and insert
the date for every weekday remaining on the academic calendar.
Under the "Reason For Casual Attire," you will see I have taken
the liberty of typing an explanation excerpted from Ralph Waldo
Emerson's seminal 1841 essay titled "Self-Reliance." In choosing
to conform and fill out the form, we will gain the liberty to choose
what we wear each day.

Dr. Olivia Green
Associate Professor of English, Clary-Smith University

Professional Attire Exception Request Form

Any faculty member requesting an exception to wear "blue jeans" to campus for academic activities must submit the following form with his or her program coordinator's signature at least two weeks in advance of the casual day. Requests that do not meet the two-week deadline will automatically be denied.

Name:_____

Department:_____

Date of Exception:_____

Reason for Casual Attire: "Society everywhere is in conspiracy against the manhood of every one of its members. ...The virtue in most request is conformity. Self-reliance is its aversion. ... I am ashamed to think how easily we capitulate to badges and names, to large societies and dead institutions."

—Ralph Waldo Emerson, "Self-Reliance"

Faculty member's initials:_____

Chairperson's signature: *Dr. Olivia Green*

LIVIE
Well … flying cooter crickets. This morning
I read Tripp McLovelace's research paper.
He was supposed to choose a social
justice issue that mattered to him and
write a research paper that explained
multiple perspectives about the topic. He
didn't submit any of the required related
assignments we have completed for the
last month. What he turned in for a graded
essay, I just discovered, is twenty pages of
the national Men's Lacrosse Rule Book. He
just copied and pasted.

ROGER
Well, at least he turned in something. That
hasn't happened in three semesters.
Dr. Green, I think you may have built some
rapport with him! Look at you meeting
students where they are.

DENISE
It makes my stomach hurt to even
think about what will be required to
handle this.

LIVIE
I called him into my office to discuss the
matter. He denies the charge. He claims
that lacrosse is "the most important justice
issue" to him, and he knows everything
there is to know about it. It is pure
coincidence that the governing body for the
sport wrote the same exact words as he did.

MERYL
Jesus fix it.

GEORGIANA
You are so good at the Honor Court, Livie. I
sure as hell wouldn't want to face off with you.

LIVIE
I hate going there, especially with
the Dean of Retention as the chair.
Every decision they make is just a
crapshoot.

GEORGIANA
Greg Rickles is a fartberry.

MERYL
Yeah, the Dean of Keeping
Students Here shouldn't chair a
committee that sometimes needs
to kick students out.

LIVIE
It is absolutely the worst part of this job.
I can only imagine how the President will
try to complicate this. I bet everybody
on the Honor Court has already had their
arms twisted. Having the kids of senior
administrators in our classes creates
so many conflicts of interest. Not in the
mood for another rodeo. I'm going home
after my 2:00 class. If the Grim Reaper
starts snooping around, tell him I'm in the
bathroom completing my three-step breast
self-exam as is required by Health Services.

To: Green, Olivia
From: McLovelace, Grady
Sent: Fri 11/12/10 10:43 p.m.

Dr. Green,

Tonight after attending my son's lacrosse game, he informed me of your conversation with him earlier today. I am disappointed to hear that you weren't satisfied with his work. He puts so much effort into balancing his academics and athletics and is incredibly hard on himself when his best effort isn't good enough. He's always been such a perfectionist, and he's really upset that you didn't like his essay. Please stop by my office next week. I would like to talk to you about how we can get around this little challenge. I am hopeful that you can extend the deadline and give Tripp the chance to rewrite his essay so that it will somehow meet your high standards.

Dr. Grady McLovelace
President, Clary-Smith University

To: McLovelace, Grady
From: Green, Olivia
Sent: Mon 11/15/10 8:03 a.m.

President McLovelace,

According to the Federal Educational Rights and Privacy Act (FERPA), no university professor is allowed to talk to anyone about a student's grades or attendance without the student's written consent. This has been the law in America since 1974.

Dr. Olivia Green
Associate Professor of English, Clary-Smith University

To: Green, Olivia
FROM: Alder, Dutch
SENT: Mon 11/15/10 10:54 a.m.

Hey Livie. I'm on the Honor Court, and I wanted to let you know that the Pres just emailed me and implicitly threatened that my program might be cut if the panel didn't rule in Tripp's favor. I share this not to dissuade you from doing the right thing. In fact, I'm looking forward to the presentation of your case tomorrow. McShitface is going to find a way to destroy the arts one way or another, and I would just as soon get canned knowing I didn't let him intimidate me. He poured the gasoline. Light the match, Doc.

Dr. Dutch Alder
Clary-Smith Art Department (All of It—It's Just Me)

To: Green, Olivia
FROM: Grim, Ronald
SENT: Mon 11/15/10 1:15 p.m.

Dr. Green,

President McLovelace just stopped by my office and informed me of your spat with his son, Tripp. Please stop by my office before you leave this evening so we can devise a strategy that will resolve this matter outside of the Honor Court and allow the student the chance to improve his standing in your course.

Dr. Ronald Grim
Dean of Humanities and Sciences, Clary-Smith University

To: Grim, Ronald
CC: Granger, Christine
FROM: Green, Olivia
SENT: Mon 11/15/10 1:36 p.m.

Dr. Grim,

I didn't have a "spat" with Tripp McLovelace. He submitted a thoroughly plagiarized draft for course credit in a freshman composition course. There is no strategy that will resolve this matter outside of the Honor Court. This case will be handled the same way all student plagiarism cases are managed by the English program: by following the protocol outlined in the Faculty Handbook. The Honor Court already has the paperwork associated with the case, and the hearing is tomorrow. I have contacted the Faculty Senate chair to let her know about the President's email to me (which encouraged me to violate FERPA guidelines) and his heavy-handed messages to members of the Honor Court in advance of the hearing. The Senate chair has been copied on this email chain as well. I will notify you about the Honor Court's verdict tomorrow.

Dr. Olivia Green
Associate Professor of English, Clary-Smith University

***

"Dr. Green, can you tell us what first aroused your suspicions about Tripp McLovelace's research paper?" asked Greg Rickles.

"I am always suspicious of any final essay that is submitted when a student has not participated in any of the required scaffolded activities that go along with it," Livie explained. "In this case, the student never submitted his thesis statement for approval. He did not write a proposal or an outline. There were four occasions when he was supposed to come to class with portions of his essay written, and he did not. He also did not participate in any of the peer revision workshops. As I began to read the essay he submitted, I recognized that his title ("Lacrosse Rules Rule!") did not match up with a social justice issue, which this paper was required to explore. It was also quite odd that the paper was twenty single-spaced pages. This only needed to be a four-page, double-spaced paper. I have never had a student in a freshman composition course write so far beyond the required length."

"What exactly are you alleging is wrong with this paper?" Rickles continued.

"Here is a copy of the American Men's Lacrosse Rule Book," Livie said, distributing the handouts to the panel. "Tripp McLovelace copied and pasted twenty pages of it and submitted it as his original work. He forgot to delete the rule and section numbers in the margins, along with the original page numbers."

"Well, did you give the student a chance to explain his approach to the assignment?" said Rickles, with skepticism in his voice.

"Indeed I did. On the morning of November 12, I emailed him and asked that he come to my office to discuss his paper," Livie said. "I asked him to explain why his essay matched the Men's Lacrosse Rule Book verbatim for twenty pages, and he could provide no satisfactory explanation. I then asked him to define several words that were included in the essay, terms like 'equidistant,' 'perpendicular,' 'longitudinal,' 'promulgated,' 'supersede,' 'asterisk,' and 'cadence' among others. He could not define any of them."

"Dr. Green, the student's defense is that your assignment expectations were unclear and that you never taught him about plagiarism. He claims he had no way to know that he was breaking a rule. How would you respond to that?" Rickles asked.

"I have several exhibits to offer here. Students were provided with a three-page written explanation of the assignment on August 30. It was accompanied by a grading rubric. Both documents were distributed in print and electronic form, and they both explain what plagiarism is. The course syllabus contains a two-page-long statement about plagiarism. We went over this statement as a class on August 16. Tripp McLovelace was present. On August 18, students signed the university's Academic Honesty contract, which reiterated the guidelines contained in the syllabus's plagiarism statement. Tripp McLovelace signed that document in class. Students were asked to read a textbook chapter about formatting, academic honesty, direct quoting, and paraphrasing for class on September 1. They used that chapter to complete academic integrity group activities on September 3 and 6. On September 27, the class embarked upon a three-day workshop devoted to learning to use MLA format to document sources. Tripp McLovelace was present on all of those class days. He also participated in a class period in the Writing Center on October 4 in which the staff talked about strategies for organizing your research process to prevent accidental plagiarism. Let me also remind the Honor Court that this is the fourth time the student has taken ENGL101. All English faculty are aligned with the same syllabus, the same assignments, and the same weekly course plans. Tripp McLovelace heard three other professors talk about the expectations for this assignment and explain academic honesty just as many times as I did."

"Dr. Green, do you think it would be possible to suspend these charges and give this student an opportunity to revise the paper?" Rickles asked.

"Absolutely not, because that option has never been extended to any other Clary-Smith student who was not the president's son. The penalty for plagiarism is failure of the course, not a do-over."

To: McLovelace, Tripp
CC: Green, Olivia
FROM: Rickles, Greg
SENT: Tues 11/16/10 3:57 p.m.

Dear Tripp,

The Honor Court has deliberated your case and found you guilty of the charge of plagiarism. The penalty is failure of your English course. Please speak with your advisor about registering for ENGL101 again in the spring semester.

Dr. Greg Rickles
Dean of Retention, Chair of the Honor Court
Clary-Smith University

***

"Considering the week you've had, I kind of wish I had more than a Nicaraguan cigar to offer. You know the men's volleyball team is in possession of the majority of the weed in a three-county radius. I'd be willing to try to get some for you," Fitz said as he swiped the fallen leaves off the two chaise lounges on the roof of the chapel.

"Now I can't have you getting defrocked helping me score," Livie laughed. "I can't smoke it anyway. Makes me paranoid. Pot turns me into the least fun person at the party. Nobody wants to hang out with the hyperventilating girl who is convinced the cops are on the way."

"Well at least the Honor Board delivered the right decision—this time," Fitz clarified. "You know, last month the chemistry department lost a case involving nine students who turned in the exact same lab report in one class. Rickles and company ruled that because the chemistry program had not explicitly written 'Students are not allowed to copy each other's lab reports' on their syllabi, the students didn't know they were breaking a rule."

"That is complete horseshit," Livie said. "The real reason was that this charge was a second offense for several of those students. A conviction would have meant expulsion, so the Honor Court ruled in their favor to keep them and their tuition here."

To: Green, Olivia
From: Caldwell, Trystyn
Sent: Mon 11/17/10 9:15 a.m.

doctor g I am missing class today because i have to be in court

To: Caldwell, Trystyn
From: Green, Olivia
Sent: Mon 11/17/10 9:46 a.m.

Trystyn,

You need to be in communication with the Dean of Students about any legal situations you might be facing.

Dr. Olivia Green
Associate Professor of English, Clary-Smith University

To: Green, Olivia
From: Caldwell, Trystyn
Sent: Mon 11/17/10 10:02 a.m.

oh no its not me it is my roommate who needs to be in court i am giving him a ride

November 17, 2010

Clary-Smith Clarion

A Covert Faculty NEWSPAPER

Because higher education is a dumpster fire, and we don't have the budget to buy extinguishers

The Clarion has learned that the Health and Safety Committee filed an injunction against Dutch Alder for allowing his art students to pollute the groundwater in Troy Lake with their art paints, an apparent violation of OSHA code 543.24 R. The man just can't catch a break.

CIS professor Dr. Stan Chu continues to struggle with the "reply all" function on his email. This is especially distressing considering he has a terminal degree in computers.

Emails from the Dean of Technological Innovation promoting his sparsely attended professional development brown bags are growing even more thirsty. It sure is a bitch trying to compel faculty to attend events that justify your job when said faculty don't believe you should have that job in the first place.

Dr. Livie Green's frustration with the business office continues. No matter which form she fills out to complete her transactions, it is never the right one, and she has to resubmit. For her latest check request, she filled out all eleven forms available on the business office website and submitted them with her application, telling Mitchell Coughlin he could shred the ones that weren't needed. It worked. When asked for comment about the ongoing situation, Dr. Green explained, "That Mitch is a complete space cadet when it comes to the athletic program overspending by the millions, but by golly, he's Dick Tracy over my $14.93 gas receipt."

Dr. Varner Earnhardt, The Dean of Assessment, won't stop using the word "aggregate" in conversation. Everything that man touches turns straight to shit, yet here we are with him in charge of our institutional data.

Somebody needs to tell Facilities Manager Frank Abbott that Business Program Chair Dr. Toby Zink hung a painting in his office with a real-life screw drilled in the wall.

To: Green, Olivia
From: Caldwell, Trystyn
Sent: Fri 11/19/10 9:43 a.m.

doctor g my right calf muscle is twitching and i need to go see the trainer i have a very important track meet this weekend

To: Caldwell, Trystyn
From: Green, Olivia
Sent: Fri 11/19/10 9:54 a.m.

Trystyn,

This will be your 9th absence. You will fail the course if you miss 10 classes.

Dr. Olivia Green
Associate Professor of English, Clary-Smith University

GEORGIANA

My Schooner says it's the Monday before Thanksgiving, and we should all climb up in a bag and hide.

LIVIE

Oh I know lots of people who should crawl up in a bag and hide.

MERYL

Let's start with Tripp McLovelace. Did you hear he got caught stealing the Angel Tree out of the lobby in the chapel? It still had the names and wish lists of the Christian Ministry kids hanging on it. He wanted a Christmas tree for his dorm room.

To: All Humanities and Sciences Faculty
From: Grim, Ronald
CC: Hillyer, Tammy Jane
Sent: Mon 11/22/10 4:30 p.m.

Colleagues,

This fall I have observed the creative ways the university has used its new tagline—"Shoot. Score. Graduate."—in a variety of settings, from the temporary tattoos of the slogan that we distributed to students, to the branded banners that were hung in the Keith Gymnasium. I think the Humanities and Sciences division is missing a tremendous opportunity to harness the same kind of energy with our own tagline, so I have scheduled a mandatory workshop for this Saturday, November 27, from 8:00 a.m. to 5:00 p.m. for us to create our own slogan. While we could work on this task after-hours during the week, I truly think it is important for us to create a dedicated space in which to work uninterrupted so that our innovative ideas can flow freely. I will bring the coffee and doughnuts!

Dr. Ronald Grim
Dean of Humanities and Sciences, Clary-Smith University

LIVIE
ON THANKSGIVING WEEKEND?
He is out of his mind.

ROGER
So much for going home to
St. Petersburg for the holiday.
Maybe I will be able to visit
Uncle Gus's grave at Christmas.

GEORGIANA
Jesus, Mary, and Joseph.

MERYL
Also, sidebar here, but how will
students wearing a temporary tattoo
underneath their clothes in late
November attract new students?

DENISE
Well, if they are hooking up with a student
from another school within 3-5 days of
tattoo application, that student might see
it before it fades. Maybe we will see a
spike in transfers.

LIVIE
You guys, I just heard from David
Miller in chemistry. I am reasonably
sure his head is going to explode.
He had tickets to the Alabama/
Auburn game this weekend with
his whole family. They are die-hard
Auburn fans. David's an alum.

GEORGIANA
Maybe if he can wait for his head to
explode until we are actually in the
workshop on Saturday, it will be canceled.

Saturday, 11/27 Humanities and Sciences Tagline Workshop Minutes

YARBROUGH BUILDING ROOM 212
NOTETAKER: DR. GEORGIANA PONSONBY, DUCHESS OF ETERNAL GRUDGES
PRESIDING: THE DEAN OF NOTHINGNESS

9:14 a.m.   The meeting starts more than an hour late.
              The Dean of Nothingness claims that Tammy
              Jane put 9:00 into his electronic calendar
              instead of 8:00. Also, he did not bring coffee
              and doughnuts as promised. Attendees realize
              this workshop will now go past 5:00 this
              evening to compensate for his ineptitude.

9:15 a.m.   The dean takes roll with an actual clipboard.
              Chances increase that somebody might get a
              wrist slapped with a ruler for misbehaving.

9:17 a.m.   Dr. Meryl Kaiser begins to grade papers. She
              has 76 freshman research essays to score this
              weekend.

9:43 a.m.   Faculty are put into small working groups
              against their will to think about how a tagline
              could function for the Humanities and
              Sciences. They are tasked with creating
              a "wish list" for the slogan's outcomes.
              Dr. Dan Anastas says he wishes one of his
              major organs would rupture because he would
              rather be hospitalized than be here right now.

9:55 a.m.   Dr. Livie Green takes a sleeve of crackers out
              of her purse. She's going to need it.

10:34 a.m.   The working groups disagree on how long a
              tagline can actually be. Thirty-six minutes
              are wasted in vigorous discussion. It is finally
              decided that 12 words or fewer is best.

10:55 a.m.   The Dean of Nothingness suggests that Dr. Dutch Alder get started on a sketch that could be used as a complement to the tagline once it is completed. Dr. Alder says he is "fundamentally opposed to graphic art for religious reasons" just to fuck with the dean's mind for a little bit.

11:58 a.m.   Anthropology professor Dr. Samantha Whitehead requests that the word "innovate" not be used because it "gives her the willies."

12:06 p.m.   Philosophy professor Dr. Bertram Kensington asks whether a single tagline can ever truly express the diverse ways of being represented by people from so many disciplines. Hope blossoms that this might be the end of the Saturday charade, but alas, the Dean of Nothingness is only temporarily delayed by the question.

12:09 p.m.   The Dean of Nothingness tells the group they have to pay for their own lunch and be back in 30 minutes. English program faculty make a plan to divide and conquer. Roger Eumenides heads to the liquor store for rum. Denise McGillicuddy drives down to the corner gas station for 5 Jumbo cups half-full of cola and ice. Meryl Kaiser calls in two pizzas. Livie Green makes a dash for a convenience store just across the county line that sells scratch-off lottery tickets.

12:39 p.m.   The meeting resumes with a 25-minute debate between Dr. Elaine Savage (Human Services) and Dr. Tyler Simmons (Environmental Science) over whether it is better to use the word "needs" or "requires."

1:34 p.m.	The loud crash of a car accident is heard out on the highway in front of the Yarbrough building. History professor Dr. Terrence Forney runs from the room claiming to know CPR, even though he really doesn't. If his book bag isn't still in Yarbrough 212 on Monday, he'll just buy another one.
2:02 p.m.	Dr. Roger Eumenides posits the idea of using the word "SQUIRREL" as an acronym to build the tagline. The group spends 15 minutes trying to come up with a suitable "Q" word, but then abandons the idea.
3:36 p.m.	Dr. Olivia Green suggests that the group just borrow a line from the classic Jimmy Buffett song "Changes in Latitudes, Changes in Attitudes."
3:38 p.m.	With momentum clearly in a stall, the Dean of Nothingness recommends that the group go outside for fresh air to clear their minds. He says that sitting in a circle under a tree might be a way to gather the force of the group's energy. Dr. Georgiana Ponsonby objects, saying that she is not holding hands and singing "Kumbaya" on a day that she isn't even supposed to be at work. Also, she hates the trees and outside.
4:04 p.m.	English faculty embark on a separate slogan creation activity, this one for their favorite celebrities. Dr. Roger Eumenides comes up with the winning tagline for actor, producer, and director William Shatner: "Don't shit the Shat." Dr. Livie Green shoots rum and cola out of her nose, and says, "It burns. It burns. It burns," a little too loud. Dr. Denise

	McGillicuddy notes how Roger's slogan artfully plays with the present and past tense of "shit" as well as hearkening back to the timeless David Hasselhoff slogan, "Don't hassle the Hoff."
5:24 p.m.	Dr. Meryl Kaiser cheers and then puts her hand over her mouth. She just won $15 in the North Carolina Education Lottery.
5:40 p.m.	English Professor Dr. Georgiana Ponsonby texts her English colleagues to ask "Is David crying?" Dr. Roger Eumenides explains that he just checked the college football scores, and Auburn came back from a 21-point deficit in the first quarter to beat Alabama by 1 in Tuscaloosa.
5:41 p.m.	Overcome with grief that he missed the action, Dr. David Miller rolls into the floor and curls up into a ball.
5:43 p.m.	Dr. Denise McGillicuddy realizes she has never been buzzed at work. Then she realizes that she never really needed to be until today.
5:55 p.m.	Dr. Burris's absolutely adorable five-year-old daughter, Tabby, comes in and says, "Mommy, is it time yet? Daddy and I have been in the car a long time. I want to go buy our Christmas tree." Even that is not enough to get Dr. Burris dismissed early, resulting in the collective realization that we are all doomed.
6:14 p.m.	The group finally decides on a tagline: "Because the world's complex problems require world-class critical thinkers." The Dean of Nothingness muses that now that

the Humanities and Sciences have a tagline,
it would be best if the individual programs
came up with their own taglines too. All
attendees let out an unrestrained groan
in unison.

6:15 p.m.   Dr. Dutch Alder points out that this exercise
required 19 faculty, 1 administrator, and 9
hours—and only yielded 10 words. He moves
that the meeting be adjourned. The vote is
unanimous before the Dean of Nothingness
has a chance to respond.

To: Humanities and Sciences Faculty
From: Grim, Ronald
Sent: Tue 11/30/10 4:57 p.m.

Colleagues,

I appreciate all of your dedicated effort at our post-Thanksgiving tagline workshop. Our day together was further proof to me that the Humanities and Sciences division is the most creative and innovative group of faculty at Clary-Smith. I did, however, receive some disappointing news from Tanya Kleinschmidt in the Public Relations Department. According to the guidelines contained in the university's style guide, no program, division, or department is allowed to have a tagline that is different from the university's official slogan. Therefore, our plans to put "Because the world's complex problems require world-class critical thinkers" on frisbees as a spring promotion will not be possible.

All the Best,
Dr. Ronald Grim
Dean of Humanities and Sciences, Clary-Smith University

DENISE
So, are we going to talk about
the tagline debacle?

ROGER
No.

GEORGIANA
No.

MERYL
No.

LIVIE
No. And I tried to make a strudel
last night, and it busted open on
me and ended up looking like a
peach-filled pastry canoe.

DENISE
Alrighty then.

DECEMBER

To: AllFaculty; AllStaff
From: Forsythe, Keesha
Sent: Wed 12/1/10 8:40 a.m.

The holiday season is one of the most stressful times of the year. With parties to host, gifts to buy, relatives making extended visits, children out of school, and unhealthy Christmas goodies tempting us around every corner, it is important to be aware of how unmanaged stress can negatively impact our health.

One of the most effective ways to mediate the effects of a stressful environment is to use a journal to actually name the aspects of your life that are threatening a healthful personal balance. You might even add a journal to your Christmas wish list when friends and family ask you what kind of gift you would like to receive. With a journal, you can practice mindfulness on a daily basis, listing the stressors that are causing you angst. Here's to a Merry Christmas and a stress-free New Year!

To Good Health,
Keesha Forsythe, RN
Clary-Smith School Nurse

GEORGIANA
You want me to list what stresses
me out? Oh, let's play this game!
Let me go first.

LIVIE
Clary-Smith's institutional identity
is built upon a disturbing level of
stress, and that makes me feel like
journaling.

DENISE
I'm disappointed. I really thought
Keesha's December post was
going to include holiday recipes
for more healthful baking. I was
counting on a good recipe for
a cookie made with applesauce
instead of butter.

MERYL
Who wants to take bets on
January's topic? I'll put five
bucks on setting healthy
New Year's resolutions.

ROGER
I'll put five on the health benefits
of drinking in moderation on
New Year's Eve. And I'll add an
extra five as a side bet that she
will recommend swapping out a
sugar-laden cocktail for a more
antioxidant-rich red wine.

GEORGIANA
She hasn't said a damn word in
any of these emails about the
importance of antioxidants, a true
cornerstone of healthy living.
That has to be in January.

To: Green, Olivia
From: Caldwell, Trystyn
Sent: Wed 12/1/10 2:24 p.m.

doctor g you are not going to believe this I OVERSLEPT THIS MORNING!!!!!!!! i am so sorry

To: Caldwell, Trystyn
From: Green, Olivia
Sent: Wed 12/1/10 2:30 p.m.

Trystyn,

This was your 10th absence, so you have failed ENGL101. I entered the grade this morning with the Registrar.

Dr. Olivia Green
Associate Professor of English, Clary-Smith University

To: Green, Olivia
FROM: Grim, Ronald
SENT: Wed 12/1/2010 4:25 p.m.

Dr. Green,

Please be advised that a student complained about you to the president. Any student issues you are having must be reported to me.

Dr. Ronald Grim, Dean of the Humanities and Sciences
Clary-Smith University

To: Grim, Ronald
FROM: Green, Olivia
SENT: Wed 12/1/2010 4:31 p.m.

Dr. Grim,

I can't report student issues to you unless the student actually tells me there is an issue. What was the nature of the complaint? What am I alleged to have done?

Also, just to confirm the chain of command so I will know how to do this, as the program coordinator, I tell the chair how I have wronged the student. Then the chair tells you. From there I wait for you to tell the chair your response, which the chair will then forward to me, correct?

Dr. Olivia Green
Associate Professor of English, Clary-Smith University

To: Green, Olivia
FROM: Grim, Ronald
SENT: Wed 12/1/2010 4:36 p.m.

Dr. Green,

You should be aware that the hostility of your tone borders on insubordination.

Dr. Ronald Grim, Dean of the Humanities and Sciences
Clary-Smith University

LIVIE
I almost got to insubordination with the dean today. I was THIS CLOSE. I was also reported to the president by a student. It was a banner day.

ROGER
Are you teaching obscene literature again?

LIVIE
That's the thing. I don't know. Grimbo won't tell me what I did, only that I'm in trouble deep. And I haven't even gotten to Allen Ginsberg yet in my lit class.

GEORGIANA
It was "Howl" that caused the uproar with that Religion student last year, right?

LIVIE
Uh huh. She just couldn't handle "cock and endless balls" in her poetry. That poem that insinuated the extramarital sex of two fictional characters earlier in the semester pushed her delicate sensibilities just about as far as they could go.

To: Green, Olivia
From: Ramsey, Kelvin
Sent: Thu 12/2/10 5:39 p.m.

Olivia,

This is Kelvin. I am concerned about my grade in Writing 2. What can I do to pull up my grade and make sure that I pass.

Kelvin Ramsey
Clary-Smith Men's Basketball Center, Class of '13

To: Ramsey, Kelvin
From: Green, Olivia
Sent: Fri 12/3/10 8:10 a.m.

Kelvin,

Two things here. Remember you need to use your professors' titles and last names to address them. We have talked about this in class a number of times.

Secondly, the dough is pretty well done on your semester because you did not submit the three major essays in the course. September would have been a better time for concern. You did not attend your individual conference with me last week. That is when I explained every student's specific course standing. Unfortunately, there are not enough points left in the class for you to pass. You actually do not even need to come and take the final exam today at 11:00 a.m., though you are certainly free to take it as a practice run for next semester.

Dr. Olivia Green
Associate Professor of English, Clary-Smith University

To: Green, Olivia
FROM: Ramsey, Kelvin
SENT: Fri 12/3/10 9:46 a.m.

I need extra credit then.

Kelvin Ramsey
Clary-Smith Men's Basketball Center, Class of '13

To: Ramsey, Kelvin
FROM: Green, Olivia
SENT: Fri 12/3/10 10:05 a.m.

Kelvin,

I do not offer extra credit. This policy is on the first page of the syllabus.

Dr. Olivia Green
Associate Professor of English, Clary-Smith University

To: Green, Olivia
FROM: Ramsey, Kelvin
SENT: Fri 12/3/10 10:22 a.m.

If I don't pass your class, my GPA won't be high enough to play basketball next year. Coach will have to bench me. I have to get some extra credit.

Kelvin Ramsey
Clary-Smith Men's Basketball Center, Class of '13

To: Ramsey, Kelvin
From: Green, Olivia
Sent: Fri 12/3/10 10:29 a.m.

Kelvin,

You should have been thinking about your playing eligibility throughout the semester when you were not submitting work. Nothing can be done to change that now, unfortunately.

Dr. Olivia Green
Associate Professor of English, Clary-Smith University

To: Green, Olivia
From: Ramsey, Kelvin
Sent: Fri 12/3/10 10:42 a.m.

You can't do this to me. I have to play.

Kelvin Ramsey
Clary-Smith Men's Basketball Center, Class of '13

To: Ramsey, Kelvin
From: Green, Olivia
Sent: Fri 12/3/10 10:56 a.m.

Kelvin,

I am not doing anything to you. You did this to yourself. This is also the end of the discussion. I have to go administer our course exam now. As I said earlier, you are free to come and take the exam as practice for next semester, but you will need to register for the course again in the spring.

Dr. Olivia Green
Associate Professor of English, Clary-Smith University

***

"I forgot to tell you that your Christmas sermon in chapel on Monday was just superb," Livie said as she buttoned her winter coat and accepted a plain old gas station cigar, seeing as how she and Fitz had smoked through his entire humidor this semester. "'The Christmas Nativity and Why God Is Not an Idea (Despite What Some Misguided Visiting Religious Professor Says)' was the perfect endcap for the semester."

"I started to dedicate it publicly to Dr. Bart Hartmann of Mount Leonia College, but I kind of felt like that might be taking it too far," Fitz explained. "I did, however, feel it necessary to share the Christmas Nativity to undo any damage that boogerface may have done to the student body. These kids need God, and it is still just stunning to me that the administration would hire someone like that as a guest speaker, considering our relationship with the church. You know, over the years, as this university has spiraled into financial disarray, the slide has so clearly coincided with the leadership's rejection of the grounding principles of the school's founders. This place was literally born out of the church. You can't just turn your back on all of that and expect to flourish. I don't think God will honor it."

"It bothers me so much to see some of the predatory things our admissions department does to get students here. Many of them don't understand the financial aid paperwork they are signing. So many are first-generation college students without educated parents to guide them through the process. And the tour guides who take prospective families around campus are being told not to show them the facilities that are in disrepair. It's beginning to feel increasingly unethical. But you know, I'm preaching to the preacher here," Livie laughed.

"Sometimes I need a good preaching to."

To: Green, Olivia
FROM: Knight, Kyle
SENT: Fri 12/3/10 6:30 p.m.

Professor Green,

One of my best players, Kelvin Ramsey, is a student in your English class. He came to see me this afternoon and was very upset. He said that you are failing him and not allowing him any extra credit to make up for a few missed assignments. Kelvin has overcome a lot in his life. I am not sure how much of his story he has told you, but it is really a miracle that he made it here. I am hoping that something can be done to help him continue his athletic career here at Clary-Smith. If you fail him, his GPA will drop below 1.5, which will make him ineligible for play.

Kyle Knight
Clary-Smith Varsity Men's Basketball Coach

To: Knight, Kyle
FROM: Green, Olivia
SENT: Fri 12/3/10 6:47 p.m.

Coach Knight,

The fact that Kelvin's GPA is hovering around 1.5 in the first place is an indication that he has been in this predicament in many classes at Clary-Smith so far. My guess is that if his past professors were polled, their experiences with him would be very similar to mine. Kelvin does not turn in assignments. I used every possible avenue at my disposal to chase after him for submissions, but he just never came through. The bottom line is that students who earn academic course credits have to complete work. Also, this situation should not have come as a surprise to either one of you. I just revisited my email inbox and counted no fewer than 21 emails I sent to Kelvin this semester updating him on his declining score, asking him to submit missing assignments, and offering extra assistance during office hours. As well, I documented 4 notices through the university's early reporting system that expressed my concern about Kelvin's performance in the class. Those messages were copied to you. The semester is over. I submitted final grades for Kelvin's course a few hours ago.

Dr. Olivia Green
Associate Professor of English, Clary-Smith University

LIVIE
My grades for the semester have been
submitted. I'm free until January.

                                          CARTER
                                    Oh that's extra good.
                                   You need a long break.

LIVIE
Tell me that story you had
started last night when Mama
called and interrupted.

                                          CARTER
                      Oh this is funny as shit. You know my friend
                      P. Curtis from high school? This past Saturday
                      morning, he was burning a stump in the ground.
                      He had to go to a Christmas party with his kids,
                    and he was just 100% sure that the fire was out. It
                     wasn't, and the wind picked up considerably while
                        he was gone. Not only was his yard set ablaze,
                      the yards of his cool neighbor, his nosey neighbor,
                       and his Sheriff's Department neighbor were on fire
                        too. It turned into a full-blown brush fire that took
                      trucks from two departments to put out. The best
                   part is that when he flew into the neighborhood on
                      two wheels and went running toward the house,
                    he forgot that he had his face painted like Rudolph
                    the Red-Nosed Reindeer at the party because his
                       kids had just begged him to. Once the fire was
                     out, he had to sign a form for the fire department
                   acknowledging his irresponsibility with live embers,
                    and he now has a permanent file with the county. If
                     there are any future arsons in the county, he will be
                     at the top of their suspect list. They took a picture
                            of him for their records and everything.

LIVIE:
And you are working to get a copy
of that photo somehow. Am I right?

                                          CARTER
                                            Well duh.

To: All Humanities and Sciences Faculty
From: Green, Olivia
Sent: Mon 12/6/10 10:45 a.m.

Colleagues,

Before you leave for the holiday, please stop by my office to contribute to the Christmas bonus we are putting together for maintenance workers Lester and Brent, who keep our offices so clean all year. Lester's wife has been very ill and out of work, so it would be an especially good time for his family to receive a monetary gift. If I am not in my office when you stop by, just slide your donation under my door.

Dr. Olivia Green
Associate Professor of English, Clary-Smith University

December 20, 2010

Clary-Smith Clarion
A Covert Faculty NEWSPAPER

Because higher education is a dumpster fire, and we don't have the budget to buy extinguishers

The Christmas season at Clary-Smith was a special kind of merry this year. It was announced on November 15 that the President's office would give Christmas bonuses to all faculty for the first time in 20 years. Our weeks of gleeful anticipation were crushed like flat rabbit roadkill on December 1 when we realized the "bonuses" were actually $25 pre-tax. The grand total of $16.14 was just enough to piss us off.

Due to the generous donation of a Music Education alum, Dr. Beth Hollins was finally able to purchase enough instruments to resurrect the Clary-Smith Ringers handbell ensemble. Their inaugural Christmas concert last Sunday, however, was thoroughly ruined with dozens of alumni and community members looking on when it was discovered that someone had used a screwdriver to remove all of the clappers from inside the bells. The theft was not discovered until the concert began, and the bells didn't go "ding." Dipp McFartface and his loser lacrosse teammates are suspected in the incident. They got a hearty laugh from the back row after they had already voiced their displeasure at having to miss an NFL divisional playoff game on television to be there and get "stupid musical activity credit" for their graduation requirement.

The Humanities and Sciences Christmas gathering was one to remember. The faculty, who were exhausted from end-of-semester grading, were disheartened to learn that the event was scheduled for December 17, the day after the university had closed for the holiday. Despite the fact that the event was billed as a "party," the Dean of Nothingness made no arrangements for refreshments and instead proclaimed the festivities a potluck. Shortly after Humanities and Sciences notetaker Dr. Georgiana Ponsonby filled her plate and began chatting with colleagues, the Dean asked where her laptop was, explaining that she was still responsible for keeping an accurate accounting of the meeting to remain in compliance with SCRAMPI in the event of a future on-campus audit from the accreditation liaison. Ponsonby was kind enough to provide the minutes to the *Clarion* staff.

12/17/10
Humanities and Sciences Christmas "Party"

MEETING CONVENED AT 12:00 P.M. IN ROOM 205 OF THE YARBROUGH HUMANITIES BUILDING

12:01 p.m.   All in attendance realize the Dean of Nothingness should have posted a sign-up sheet to ensure there would be a variety of foods at the potluck. The buffet included the following: 96 red plastic cups, 1 liter of room-temperature diet ginger ale, 24 spoons, 36 paper appetizer plates with a Thanksgiving motif clearly purchased on clearance this very morning, 16 tins of Danish butter cookies, 8 pieces of cold grocery store fried chicken, a very old plastic container filled with questionable guacamole (which turned out to be a non-issue because there were no chips available to eat it with), and a pint of Dr. Livie Green's grandmother's absolutely unbelievable potato salad.

12:02 p.m.   Dr. Javier Arias hurries into the party late wearing a light-up Christmas tree hat that is finishing up the chorus of "Jingle Bells." He jerks it off his head when he realizes he was mistaken in thinking that festive attire was required. He is heard muttering "damn it all to hell" as he tries unsuccessfully to get the lights to stop flashing.

12:05 p.m.   Tammy Jane Hillyer lights two of Becky McLovelace's miserable Frosty Winter Wonderland candles, creating a toxic cloud of vanilla smog that renders the eastern end of the room completely uninhabitable.

The noxious fragrance overwhelms several faculty members, sending them in retreat to the restroom with burning eyes. Likewise, the odor triggers Dr. Dutch Alder's asthma, forcing him into the hallway to puff on his inhaler.

12:06 p.m.   Tammy Jane opens several windows and apologizes profusely for exposing the group to such a hazard, claiming she "just had no idea a candle could go so wrong."

12:09 p.m.   Mamaw's tater salad is G-O-N-E. For many, this was their only reason to stay. The crowd thins considerably.

12:15 p.m.   Lots of forced, uncomfortable chitchat. Very uncomfortable indeed.

12:20 p.m.   Dr. Jim Culp's bitterness about having to provide food for a Christmas party escalates the more he thinks about it. He gripes that he isn't wasting an afternoon on this thing next year unless there is a caterer. And he's taking his unopened tin of Danish butter cookies home, damn it.

12:21 p.m.   Despite vigorous protests, the Dean of Nothingness forces faculty to play the Christmas balloon pop game. Festive balloons are tied to the ankle of each professor. The object of the game is to stomp on and thus pop the other players' balloons and get them out while also protecting one's own balloon. The notetaker does not think this is a game that uncoordinated academics should be playing. The prize—a new stapler and 3-hole punch set—is also not worth the physical exertion.

12:24 p.m.   Dr. Dutch Alder is loaded into the back seat of Dr. Roger Eumenides's Honda Civic for a ride to the emergency room and an X-ray of his ankle.

12:40 p.m.   This party is somehow still happening. The Dean of Nothingness will not let it die.

12.59 p.m.   Update from the ER: Dr. Alder's ankle is indeed broken. He will consult with an orthopedic surgeon next week about potential surgery.

1:06 p.m.   Dr. Livie Green shares the good news that she has just finished composing the Writing Center Annual Report and fall 2010 attendance was up 35% from the previous semester. Instead of congratulating her and complimenting the staff, the Dean of Nothingness reminds Green that he needs to preview a full spreadsheet with the data before any findings are announced publicly.

1:13 p.m.   Dr. Anna Cox from the history department pushes Dr. Green a second time for her potato salad recipe. Green politely declines, stating that it is a recipe her dead grandmother insisted should stay in the family. Cox is livid.

1:18 p.m.   The Dean of Nothingness announces his Christmas gift to faculty: 10 free photocopies. Dr. Kaiser does the math in her head and realizes that if the entire division pooled their free photocopies, they could print the spring syllabus for a single course.

1:23 p.m.   Utterly exhausted from marathon grading, Dr. Denise McGillicuddy returns from taking a nap on the couch in her office. For the last hour, she has been setting her alarm: 10 minutes of sleep, 10 minutes of party.

1:25 p.m.   Tammy Jane presents the Dean of Nothingness with her Christmas gift: a completely red 750-piece jigsaw puzzle that will likely keep the dipshit occupied for the whole month of January so she can actually get some work done.

1:29 p.m.   In closing up the party, the Dean of Nothingness tells faculty that the Board of Trustees meets tomorrow and will probably vote to suspend the university's retirement match. Several low-enrollment majors in the Humanities are also in danger of being eliminated, though he declines to name specific areas of concern. Merry Christmas to all, and to all a good night.

To: All Humanities and Sciences Faculty
From: Hillyer, Tammy Jane
Sent: Mon 12/20/10 8:12 a.m.

Colleagues,

I am organizing a Meal Train for Dutch Alder over the holidays. The emergency room confirmed that his ankle is broken following the Humanities and Sciences Christmas party. He is not going to be mobile for at least a few weeks. If you would like to participate in taking him a meal, please let me know so I can add you to the schedule.

Tammy Jane Hillyer
Administrative Assistant to the
Dean of Humanities and Sciences

DENISE
All right, Livie. I don't
understand your Christmas gift.

GEORGIANA
I was just about to text the
same thing. Why is there a
single puzzle piece in this box?

LIVIE
Lester and Brent, the maintenance
workers, let me into Grim's office very
early one morning last week. You
are now the owners to the missing
puzzle pieces in each of four Grim
puzzles. Take them as a token of
my appreciation of your work in this
department and as a reminder of him
crawling around under his desk looking
for them when the time comes.

MERYL
AAAAAAAH. I love it!

ROGER
Hahahahaha! All hail Livie Green.

To: Green, Olivia
FROM: Berry, Elizabeth
SENT: Tue 12/21/10 8:49 a.m.

Dr. Green,

I know it's almost Christmas, but I need a big favor. It's a really long shot, but there's this paid summer internship at the White House that I've always wanted to apply for, but I've made it to my junior year and haven't done it yet. I procrastinated on applying because my family thinks I'm being ridiculous. They want me to get a summer job at the grocery store near my house. However, I know I'll regret it if I don't at least try for the internship. It even includes housing, which is a huge deal in DC. Is there any chance you would have time to write a recommendation letter for me by December 31st?

Sincerely,
Elizabeth Berry

To: Berry, Elizabeth
FROM: Green, Olivia
SENT: 12/21/10 10:02 a.m.

Hi, Liz. Of course I will write the letter, and of course you should try for this internship. You are such a bright student, and I love that you are taking aim at the long shots. Your grades are stellar and will speak for themselves. I will write a letter that will get the selection committee's attention. I am so excited about the possibilities for you—whether it is with this opportunity or the next one down the line.

Dr. Olivia Green
Associate Professor of English, Clary-Smith University

JANUARY

To: AllFaculty; AllStaff
From: Forsythe, Keesha
Sent: Mon 1/3/11 8:02 a.m.

As we move through this frigid winter at Clary-Smith, it is important to remember that even though the temperature is cold outside, we still need to take time to get out every day for some fresh air. Studies have shown that as little as 10 minutes a day of fresh air can improve your digestion, balance your blood pressure, and boost your immune system. If you find that the nip in the air is too much, try layering your clothing and adding gloves and a scarf.

To Good Health,
Keesha Forsythe, RN
Clary-Smith School Nurse

LIVIE
The pearls of wisdom are just raining down from Health Services today.

ROGER
Shit! Nothing about New Year's drinking?

GEORGIANA
And not a damn word about antioxidants. This is just bordering on irresponsible at this point.

MERYL
I would have never thought to put on gloves and a scarf if I was cold.

January 4, 2011

Clary-Smith Clarion
A Covert Faculty NEWSPAPER

Because higher education is a dumpster fire, and we don't have the budget to buy extinguishers

Dr. Beth Hollins's meticulous preparations for the music program's accreditation site visit this spring were thwarted yet again by greater-than-expected rainfall in December. Hollins returned from the Christmas break to discover mushrooms growing out of the baseboards of the band room. Moisture also seeped into the grand piano, causing the inner workings of the instrument to swell and not work. Hollins revealed that the woodwind instruments that were not taken home for the holidays by students are now "all fucked up," and there is no funding to make the costly instrument repairs. Music faculty knew that decades of deferred building maintenance, the result of the administration not valuing their program, would eventually catch up, and it appears that 2011 is the year they are going to have to pay the piper.

The Clarion has learned that Dr. Dutch Alder's bimalleolar ankle fracture sustained in the Christmas balloon pop game at the Humanities and Sciences holiday party late last month will not be covered as a Workman's Comp claim because the university was technically closed for break the day before the party took place. Human Resources informed Alder that he would have to work with the school nurse to file his $65,000 surgery claim through the university's abysmal insurance plan.

The president's beagle, Harvey McLovelace, continues to wreak havoc on all who work on the first floor of the administration building. Harvey's incessant barking is responsible for the Valium prescriptions of three staff members, including the president's secretary, Jill Pepper. Pepper explains, "All I hear all day is Bark. 'Harvey no.' Bark. 'Harvey no.' Bark. 'Harvey no.' Bark. 'Harvey no.' Bark. 'Harvey no.' Bark. 'Harvey no.' Bark. 'Harvey no.' Bark. 'Harvey no.' Bark. 'Harvey no.' Bark. 'Harvey no.' Bark. 'Harvey no.' And so on and so forth. It never dawns on the man that Harvey isn't listening, nor is he ever going to listen. I promise that dog will be responsible for snapping my very last nerve one day." Despite the fact that the president's office underwent a sweeping renovation in 2009, you would never know it by looking at the space now. Harvey has gnawed the door frames and the legs of the president's conference table and clawed at the wallpaper. And as this reporter types these troublesome details, it becomes apparent that both Harvey and Tripp McLovelace have been parented in much the same way. Harvey is allowed to take a dump in the hallway leading to the Advancement suite, and Tripp is allowed to run the Admissions golf cart into Troy Lake. Apparently when you are a McLovelace, Clary-Smith is just your playground.

Criminal justice professor Powell Parker, known on campus as the "fridge Nazi" for his insistence that expired food be promptly removed from the faculty lounge refrigerator, has recently learned that HR will not accept grievance filings against suspected rule breakers. If they did not label their food, formal action cannot be taken. Give 'em hell, Powell.

Dr. Roger Eumindes in the English program split his "blue-jean style" pants while teaching yesterday, and the exposure revealed that he was wearing Pearl Jam boxer shorts. The distress that his students didn't know the band was even greater than the embarrassment that they saw his undies.

Division of Humanities and Sciences Meeting with Dr. Gladys Myers, Dean of Institutional Research

JANUARY 7, 2010 6:00 P.M.

AGENDA
SCRAMPI OVERVIEW
DECENNIAL REVIEW PREPARATION
FACULTY TASKS

***

"I would like to thank you all for staying late on a Friday evening to discuss the very important matter of our university's accreditation," Dr. Grim began. "I know what Doctor Myers has to say to us tonight is critical to Clary-Smith's future, so I ask that you give her your undivided attention."

"So as we prepare for our decennial review, I wanted to talk to you about some housekeeping that the institution needs to take care of in order to be successful in its quest for re-accreditation," said Myers. "Our accrediting body, SCRAMPI, expects a comprehensive report—hundreds of pages—every ten years that responds to numerous standards of excellence we are required to follow. Two of those major standards relate to institutional planning and assessment. Essentially, by demonstrating the way that individuals and programs plan and then using those plans within the assessment loop to evaluate courses, we are able to successfully achieve the most important institutional goal within the decennial review: document ongoing progress."

Livie Green revved up her engine. "Oh, so, for the past ten years, the university's administration has been documenting institutional planning and assessment in preparation for this massive review."

"Well ..." Myers waffled.

"Doctor Green, you have to recognize that the deans have a tremendous load of other responsibilities," Grim interjected pointedly.

ROGER
Like working jigsaw puzzles of the horses that have won the Kentucky Derby.

"Institutional Research is admittedly just a little bit behind," Myers conceded. "I am here tonight to outline what we are requesting from faculty. First, we need you to write individual goals for the year and enter them into the online system we have created, which I will teach you tonight. Then you will enter a mid-year update that explains how you are proceeding with those goals. Finally, at the end of the year, you will write a summation that demonstrates that you met all of your goals. In the interest of time, the Institutional Research staff took the liberty of writing your 2011 to 2012 goals for you so that you can see what strong goals actually look like."

"You wrote our goals for us?" said Dutch Alder, unable to hide the astonishment in his voice.

"That is correct," admitted Myers. "However, the exciting news is that you get to be creative with the goals that come before that."

"Before that? What do you mean?" asked Georgiana Ponsonby.

"We are going to need your individual goals reports for academic years 2010 to 2011, 2009 to 2010, '08 to '09, '07 to '08, '06 to '07, '05 to '06, and '04 to '05," Myers announced.

"For the sake of clarity here, we are to go back in time to make up goals for years that have already passed?" Ponsonby said.

"Yes. By accessing this wonderfully user-friendly online portal that we have worked with IT to create," said Myers.

"Isn't that fraud?" Dr. Green asked, the tension rising in her voice.

"Doctor Green, please let Doctor Myers finish her presentation," Grim scolded.

Myers went on. "So, once you have those seven years documented, it will be time to move on to the program goals. Each of your academic programs will need to write departmental goals and student learning outcomes for the last seven years. These will need to be complete with the assessments you used—whether those were tests, essays, or other assignments—to show that the goals you set each year were achieved."

Dutch rejoined the fray. "We need tests and papers to prove we met goals seven years ago—except we are just now writing those goals? Does Institutional Research have enough in its budget to rent time machines?"

"Why are you just now telling us that this information was necessary?" Livie asked. "Whose job was it to know the SCRAMPI requirements and plan for what they would expect from us each year? Is that the dean of university planning? The dean of institutional research?"

"There is good news here too," Myers stammered. "Institutional Research staff members have already gone into the portals and written your student learning outcomes for each year."

"Your staff of non-teaching faculty determined what the academic goals of my discipline's curriculum should be?" Georgiana shouted.

"Colleagues. Please. Let Doctor Myers finish," Grim pleaded.

It was too late, though. The chorus of faculty voices rose.

"How much trouble will we be in if we are caught manufacturing these documents retroactively?"

"Some of our programs are comprised of faculty who have only been here for two or three years. How are they supposed to make up data for years that they weren't even employed by the university?"

"This portal link doesn't work. I keep clicking on it, and it says, 'Error 432.'"

"Same for me. 'Error 432.'"

"How am I supposed to get papers and tests from students who graduated seven years ago? I don't even know where they live."

LIVIE
Clary-Smith's institutional
identity is BUILT UPON
QUICKSAND, and that makes me
feel LIKE GOING HOME NOW.

CARTER
Working in real estate appraisal as long
as I have, you are bound to see some
things. I was not at all prepared for today.

LIVIE
What happened? Are you okay?

CARTER
I was out in the country looking for an address,
and it was all dirt roads with no numbers on the
mailboxes. I thought I was on the right road. The
guy told me it would curve around several times
and go about a mile and a half out through the
trees. When I had gone about two miles and still
wasn't to the house, I knew I was in the wrong
place. I was trying to turn around when I saw it ...
it was an actual still. I had never seen one in real
life before. And that's when they saw me ...two
wooly-boogers in overalls who popped up behind
it with shotguns pointed straight at me.

LIVIE
OH MY GOD! They could have killed
you, and we would have never
found your body. Don't you dare
tell Mama. She'll never let either
one of us go anywhere ever again.

***

"Hi, Doctor Green. My name is Destiny Rayburn. I just added the class yesterday, and you emailed the syllabus last night."

"Oh, yes. It's nice to meet you, Destiny," Livie said, noticing the line of students at her lectern would likely make her late for her next class. "Do you have any questions about the syllabus since you missed the first day of class?"

"I do, actually," she said, lowering her voice. "I know the textbook for the course is only nineteen dollars … but I don't have the money, and my family isn't going to have the money. Should I just drop the course and try to find a class that does not require a textbook? I love writing, and I hate I can't stay because this class sounds fun." The embarrassment on Destiny's face was heart-wrenching.

"Oh, honey, no. You don't have to drop the course," Livie said. "We can definitely work something out."

That's when Livie heard "excuse me" from the student behind Destiny in line. "I don't mean to butt in, Doctor G., but I was staying after class to tell you I needed to drop the course. It's not going to work out with my schedule. I got the book free from a friend in my dorm who took the class last semester. She can have it if it will help," Johnny Brooks said, handing the book to her.

Nobody spoke for a few seconds. Livie had never witnessed such an act of kindness between students before, and she let the moment wash over her.

"Welcome to the course, Destiny, and thank you, Johnny," Livie said. "I hope you both have a wonderful semester."

LIVIE
I have taken Roger off of this text chain for reasons that will become obvious in a moment. Since I am a few years older than you, I feel the need to warn you about something. As you age, your pubic hair begins to spread out to your legs. And I don't mean a little bit. Since puberty, your pubes have behaved themselves and stayed right in their lane. Then bam—one day they decide to color outside the lines. I discovered this a few days ago and was poking around down there when I also discovered my first gray hair. Not only that, one side of my labia has all of a sudden decided to sag. I mean it's like my whole vaginal area has just thrown in the towel and given up.

DENISE
This is utterly horrifying.

GEORGIANA
I just rolled out of my office chair laughing.

MERYL
Roger has privates too. I feel like he should be notified as well.

January 10, 2011

Clary-Smith Clarion
A Covert Faculty NEWSPAPER

Because higher education is a dumpster fire, and we don't have the budget to buy extinguishers

BREAKING NEWS:
CAMPUS ON LOCKDOWN AFTER BOMB SCARE

Yesterday's campus-wide lockdown was the first in the institution's history. After some sleuthing, the Clarion staff discovered the cause. Dr. Sarah Baker, recently returned from maternity leave and still struggling with the loss of brain cells in her postpartum funk, accidentally left her breast pump in the seating area outside the Provost's office. A passing maintenance worker, seeing all the tubes and cords sticking out of the mysterious bag, mistook it for a potentially dangerous package and called the authorities. While Dr. Baker is thoroughly humiliated, the chaos that ensued when the emergency alert was issued made it abundantly clear that the peckerwoods in charge of this institution are not ready for a real crisis. We need more practice and a plan.

To: Green, Olivia
FROM: Thornburg, Kaycee
SENT: Mon 1/18/11 3:10 a.m.

Doctor Green,

I saw my grade on my homework assignment. Why did you give me a C? I mean I worked so hard on that assignment. A C is just ridiculous.

Kaycee

To: Thornburg, Kaycee
FROM: Green, Olivia
SENT: Mon 1/18/11 8:22 a.m.

Kaycee,

Every grade that you are assigned in my course (even for small homework assignments) will come with written feedback and explanation in the comments section of the grading system. Look there first and let me know if you have any further questions.

Dr. Olivia Green
Associate Professor of English, Clary-Smith University

DENISE
I feel like a bag of busted buttholes today. I
wore my bedroom slippers to class because
I didn't have the energy to put on anything
else. They look enough like regular shoes that
I thought I could get away with it. When I
walked into my freshman writing class, clearly
looking like death was upon me, a student in
the back row raised his hand and asked, "Are
those your bedroom shoes?"

GEORGIANA
Oh no. I have homemade soup in the fridge.
Let me share. I'll go warm it up for you.

LIVIE
Poor Denise. Go home and rest. The Grim
Reaper is in the Deans' Council meeting this
afternoon. It will end about 2:30, and he will
be so pooped from four hours on campus that
he will leave from there. He will never know
you are gone.

January 20, 2011

Clary-Smith Clarion
A Covert Faculty NEWSPAPER

Because higher education is a dumpster fire, and we don't have the budget to buy extinguishers

Monday was the first day on the job for Clary-Smith's new Dean of Compliance, Dr. Perry Pipkin. In just a week's time, however, Dr. Pipkin earned his new nickname: The Dean of Awkward Pauses. If you see him around, ask him a question:

You: "Hi, Dr. Pipkin. How are you today?"

One Mississippi. Two Mississippi. Three Mississippi. Four Mississippi. Five Mississippi.

Him: I'm fine, and I hope you are.

Clarion staff reached out to several sources to find out exactly what a Dean of Compliance does, and nobody was really sure.

Faculty in the Yarbrough building are being advised to stay away from the first-floor women's bathroom between the hours of 9:00 and 10:00 a.m. on Monday, Wednesday, and Friday. Dr. Patricia Vogel in the Sports Management department always drops a deuce after her 8:00 Global Perspectives in Sports class, and at this point on her overly zealous health journey, all she is eating is nuts and berries she forages on her mountain hikes. Her logs smell worse than a Pretty Perfections Toasted Campfire Marshmallow candle, and holy crap, that is saying a lot.

Despite the fact that all ENGL101 and 102 courses visit the Writing Center each semester to learn about the services offered by the consultants, students continue to try to drop off their papers so someone can "fix" them. The staff keeps asking Writing Center Director Livie Green if she will let one of them dress up as "The Grammar Fairy" with a pink tutu and a sequined wand. Whenever students attempt the fix-it drop-off, The Grammar Fairy could jump out from behind a filing cabinet ready to sprinkle magic dust over the essay. So far, Green is not on board, though she commends them for their creative thinking.

Reimbursement checks from the business office aren't taking 2–3 months—at this point they have stopped altogether. This means the university has blown through its cash from tuition revenue. Faculty need to begin asking some very specific questions during the public reports of senior leadership to get to the bottom of this.

Students, faculty, staff, and alumni are distressed by Dr. Jim Culp's new haircut. It's a look that has "I did it myself" written all over it. Bad. News. Bears.

LIVIE
ELIZABETH BERRY GOT THE
WHITE HOUSE INTERNSHIP!!!

GEORGIANA
Oh my God. Wow.

ROGER
Now that is a Flying Squirrel
actually flying. Unbelievable.

To: Green, Olivia
From: Thornburg, Kaycee
Sent: Sun 1/24/11 4:24 a.m.

Doctor Green,

I just saw my grade on my second homework assignment. Another C? Really?

Kaycee

To: Thornburg, Kaycee
From: Green, Olivia
Sent: Mon 1/25/11 8:02 a.m.

Kaycee,

As I mentioned in my email response about your first assignment, the justification for the grade is in the comments section beside your score. In this instance, you did not follow the assignment instructions. You were supposed to write an outline using the format on the handout we went over in class. Two sentences is not an outline. That C was a gift.

Dr. Olivia Green
Associate Professor of English, Clary-Smith University

To: AllFaculty; AllStaff
FROM: Taylor, Gloria
SENT: Fri 1/28/11 4:59 p.m.

Colleagues,

I wanted to provide an update on our Fall 2011 projected enrollment based on recent data that I received from Ramona Pfizer. Our number of deposits for incoming students compared to this date last year is down 43 percent. This means that we are going to have to make adjustments to the proposed budget for the 2011–12 academic year. More updates will be provided in the coming weeks about additional Admissions events that will hopefully attract new students.

Dr. Gloria Taylor,
Provost, Clary-Smith University

January 29, 2011

Clary-Smith Clarion
A Covert Faculty NEWSPAPER

Because higher education is a dumpster fire, and we don't have the budget to buy extinguishers

At the January meeting of the Curriculum Board, it was revealed that the administration (in concert with athletics) would like to remove the catalog protection that keeps the 11:00 a.m. chapel hour on Mondays safe from any classes or meetings being scheduled at that time. The reservation of the 11:00 hour on Monday makes it impossible for MWF classes to be scheduled at that time. This tradition of making the worship time sacred has been part of the university since its founding in 1878, and the faculty really should stand against the proposed change, especially considering that it is being made so that athletic coaches can have more uninterrupted sporting time with their athletes after they have gotten through with their pesky courses in the morning. Please stay tuned for more information and opportunities for action.

Sexual harassment continues to be poorly investigated and even more poorly handled at Clary-Smith. Take the case of Residence Life Assistant Director Susie Barrett, who has endured unwanted sexual remarks from a student for nearly a year. Instead of providing real protection—or better yet removing the student from campus altogether—Human Resources Director Denny Harper gave Barrett an actual golf club to keep in her office to help her feel more safe in case the verbal abuse escalates to physical violence.

Provost Gloria Taylor has been taking some heat recently after announcing that disappointing fall enrollments will result in budget cuts. The rumor mill has been abuzz about which areas will likely receive the brunt of the trimming, and Taylor has not been spoken of kindly. Make no mistake, though. With McShitface at the helm, Gloria Taylor is the only thing standing between us and certain disaster on any given day.

Word from the music program is that their new adjunct probably won't be back to teach in the fall, seeing as how students have been reporting his "periodic fits of rage." Granted, if we were being paid $776 after taxes to teach a 5-month course that required a significant commute from home, we'd be mad too.

PSA: If you put a note on your office door that says, "Be back in a few minutes," nobody will ever know that you are taking a nap, and they won't knock because they think you aren't there. The more you know ...

FEBRUARY

To: AllFaculty; AllStaff
From: Forsythe, Keesha
Sent: Mon 2/7/11 8:33 a.m.

As Valentine's Day approaches and you begin to think about gifts for your loved ones, don't forget there are a lot of hidden health dangers in common Valentine's Day gifts. The following guidelines will help you choose the perfect health-conscious treat for your loved ones.

Try swapping traditional chocolate candies full of fat, sugar, and preservatives with an organic fruit arrangement.

A high-calorie dinner in a fancy restaurant will not only hit your wallet, but it will also affect your waistline. Instead, make a romantic dinner at home—perhaps a nice grilled salmon and some asparagus.

Avoid floral arrangements that often contain flowers that are toxic and deadly for pets and opt instead for a handmade card that expresses your true feelings for your partner.

These easy trades can make your Valentine's Day happier and healthier!

To Good Health,
Keesha Forsythe, RN
Clary-Smith School Nurse

GEORGIANA
There. Is. Nothing. Romantic.
About. Asparagus.

LIVIE
Valentine's chocolate is the only thing that
pulls me through the 28 frozen days of the
hell known as February. And I will claw your
eyeballs out the day after Valentine's Day if
you get in my way at the 50% off sale.

MERYL
Who knew Valentine's Day was
fraught with so many perils?

ROGER
What is the school
nurse's endgame here?

GEORGIANA
One day soon, I'm going to let my
monkeys fly and respond to one
of these emails.

February 10, 2011

Clary-Smith Clarion
A Covert Faculty NEWSPAPER

Because higher education is a dumpster fire, and we don't have the budget to buy extinguishers

As much as we hate to report it, Clarion staff members hear that the Political Science program is in grave danger of cancellation. At this pace, the liberal arts will be effectively extinguished by graduation.

Sources in the Advancement office tell us that staff members are courting potential donors Eustis and Birdie Bettencourt for a sizable donation that could result in a new business program building emblazoned with the Bettencourt name. God only knows whose souls are being sold to the devil to make that deal happen.

Dr. Warren Wentz, the Dean of Service Learning, continues to waste so much time at the beginning of meetings with mindless chatter that he always runs out of time for everything else on the agenda. People with graduate degrees apparently lose their ability to manage a meeting once they matriculate. There's just no other explanation for it.

Despite the fact that the campus community has had more than a month to adjust to the newly installed speed bump leading to the faculty parking lot beside the library, students have reported that Professor McJuicington continues to struggle to remember it is there. On Tuesday, after exiting State Road 42 and failing to slow down, he hit the hump at a high rate of speed, knocking the bumper clean off of his 1980 Toyota Tercel. The student who witnessed the incident said seeing him catch air in that little car was "some shit."

English Professor Meryl Kaiser is teaching one of those ENGL102 sections where no amount of engaged pedagogy can overcome her students' unwillingness to learn. After requiring students to read a short chapter about parallelism, complete practice exercises, and then discuss them in class, her quiz question in the next period—What is parallelism?—was still a total belly-flop. Eleven students responded with the predictable "I don't know" or "IDK." One respondent suggested that parallelism was a math equation, while another more creative student guessed that it might have something to do with going to paralegal school. This is college now.

The Provost's recent email announcing the Admissions department's abysmal recruiting season mentioned additional prospective student events that will draw incoming scholars. Faculty are taking bets about exactly how students will be coddled and babied. Guesses include piñata games, a mime, funnel cakes, and a slime-making station.

DENISE
You guys. I just taught ethos,
pathos, and logos to my freshman
composition students, and it
was one of the best classroom
experiences of my entire career.
They totally got it. We had synergy.
I can't even describe the feeling.

LIVIE
Well done, Dr. McGillicuddy! I'm convinced
that what we're doing in these classrooms
each day with these students is the only
thing right about this institution.

GEORGIANA
We have to celebrate the victories.

MERYL
Always.

To: AllFaculty
From: McLovelace, Grady
Sent: Mon 2/14/11 4:59 p.m.

The Clary-Smith Board of Trustees is sad to report that after 102 years of continuous operation, the political science program is closing. Despite this loss, Clary-Smith will strive to demonstrate its commitment to the liberal arts. The Director of Student Activities is already searching for event speakers for the coming year that will discuss political issues and thus ensure that Clary-Smith students have an opportunity to explore both national and world events.

As this door of the institution's past closes, the Board of Trustees is excited to announce that Clary-Smith plans to pursue a Master of Science in Nursing program, the first graduate program in the school's history. The program, which will be housed in the new Lucas Rude Health Sciences Building, will come before the faculty for a vote in March, with a proposed opening date of Fall 2013.

Dr. Grady McLovelace
President, Clary-Smith University

February 15, 2011

Clary-Smith Clarion
A Covert Faculty NEWSPAPER

Because higher education is a dumpster fire, and we don't have the budget to buy extinguishers

With the demise of the Dance, Drama, Foreign Language, and Political Science programs in just the last few months, the Humanities at Clary-Smith have been put on alert: your major could be the next one. You can count on the Clarion's staff for up-to-the-minute reporting about any other impending closures. Our "slanderous" and "subversive" reporting has been spot on so far.

Faculty were also surprised to learn from the Board of Trustees that a planned opening date for the new Master's in Nursing program has already been set, even though the faculty haven't even seen a draft of the curricular proposal. If it does pass, there is no doubt the faculty and students in the new Health Sciences building will enjoy the best that Clary-Smith has to offer. The building plans boast four floors of state-of-the-art classrooms equipped with the latest medical simulators and technologies. Every student seat is equipped with a tablet, a phone charger, and outlets for other devices, and faculty in each classroom space will have access to interactive whiteboards on every wall. The front desk in the building's lobby will be staffed forty hours per week by a "concierge," who can provide directions for those who are looking for a specific location, or make photocopies for busy faculty and staff. Even the elevators will contain flat-screen televisions showing a reel of footage about the hands-on clinical experiences students in the health sciences enjoy. Every faculty member who teaches in the building will be issued a new computer that is compatible with the interactive whiteboards, and new photocopy machines will be installed on every floor. Health sciences faculty will be issued a copy code that will allow them to make unlimited photocopies. A recent Clarion survey of faculty developed after the announcement of the specifics of the Rude building yielded a list of questions that will be taken to the Faculty Senate for clarification:

1. One of my classrooms still has a chalkboard, and with academic budgets frozen, I can't even get chalk. Will it be possible for Nursing faculty to use their budgets to buy us chalk?

2. Is it true that there will be a Starbucks in the lobby of the new Health Sciences building? If so, will the lowly faculty in other buildings be allowed to come in, or will that coffee be reserved for the Health Sciences faculty?

3. Will the 10-photocopy limit for faculty and staff across campus be lifted once the Nursing faculty are allowed unlimited copies on their new machines?

4. When it rains and my Monday/Wednesday/Friday 9:00 classroom floods, will I be allowed to take my students to the Health Sciences building to stay dry?

5. Can the Senate confirm that the salaries of the new Master's in Nursing faculty will be three times the salary of the highest-paid faculty member outside of that discipline?

6. There are mushrooms growing out of the baseboards in my main teaching space. I have been on the Facilities repair waiting list for a year and a half for other neglected maintenance issues. Can these things be addressed before a new building is constructed?

7. The Senate chair stopped buying name-brand juice bottles for faculty meetings, and the off-brand has too much pulp. I formally request that name-brand juices be restored to the buffet.
8. If the faculty decides to reject the forthcoming Master of Science in Nursing curricular proposal, can the Business program have the fourth floor of the Health Sciences building?

To: Green, Olivia
From: Thornburg, Kaycee
Sent: Tue 2/15/11 2:45 a.m.

Doctor Green,

I just logged in and saw the grade you gave me on my rhetorical analysis draft. I shouldn't be surprised at this point considering the way you grade, but I'm not going to let you give me an F. This is totally unfair.

Kaycee

To: Thornburg, Kaycee
From: Green, Olivia
Sent: Tue 2/15/11 8:55 a.m.

Kaycee,

As always, the explanation is in the comments section. You failed because you submitted the assignment 8 days late. The syllabus outlines the policies for late work. I suggest you review that document.

I also recommend that you revisit the email etiquette handout we went over in the first week of class. Remember that emailing professors about grades (particularly when you are upset) is not a good strategy. Instead, you should request a meeting so the issue can be discussed in person.

Dr. Olivia Green
Associate Professor of English, Clary-Smith University

To: AllFaculty; AllStaff
From: Harper, Denny
Sent: Tue 2/15/11 10:59 a.m.

Dear Colleagues,

The National Weather Service has its eye on a winter storm that could impact our region of North Carolina with up to two inches of snow this time next week. The senior leadership team is watching the forecast, and our maintenance crews are already gearing up for a winter weather event. Remember, any cancellations or delays will be communicated through the university's emergency alert system. If you have questions or concerns, please reach out to Human Resources.

Denny Harper
Human Resources Director, Clary-Smith University

FITZ
I'm already in prayer.
Snowpocalypse 2011 is upon us.
This place is going to grind to a
screeching halt, and the masses
will descend into utter panic.

LIVIE
Alert! Alert! Alert! The National
Weather Service is now talking about
the possibility of THREE inches!

FITZ
The Lord be with you.

LIVIE
And with you.

February 16, 2011

Clary-Smith Clarion

A Covert Faculty NEWSPAPER

Because higher education is a dumpster fire, and we don't have the budget to buy extinguishers

Faculty Development funding is the first casualty of the projected budget shortfall. Effective immediately, no funding will be approved for faculty travel to academic conferences. However, budget woes didn't stop Soccer Coach Champ Rialto from taking the entire soccer team all the way to Florida to play exactly two matches (with a day off in between for rest and a visit to Florida's newest waterpark). The university won't fund faculty's academic travel, but the soccer team can splash away on Clary-Smith's dime.

It's that time of year once again: Homecoming 2011 is already brewing. That can only mean one thing: the Advancement office is gearing up for the avalanche of complaints from the impossible to satisfy fuddy-duddy alums from the 1950s and '60s.

"Crazy Bill," the whack-a-doodle fundamentalist preacher from Hickory Grove, continues to use the university's "Free Speech Zone" at the campus clock tower to exercise his First Amendment right to cause an inordinate amount of trouble. Lately he has taken to screaming "Hell burns hot for whores" at the female students who pass by on their way to class. They are all facing eternal damnation for either their makeup, their pants, or their desire to work outside the home.

This week several deans have been spotted in their offices before 10:00 a.m., sparking speculation that something is amiss. The mystery was solved Monday when emails were sent to all program chairs asking for them to add more 8:00 a.m. classes to the Fall 2011 course schedule, even though we all know the students will not register for classes that early, and the professors who get stuck with those sections will have their entire schedules screwed when they are canceled and rescheduled. We do the dance, though, because they call the shots.

Please stop by the library this week to make a purchase at the annual book sale. The librarians donate editions from their own personal collections to raise money to pay for the photocopies that students can't afford throughout the year. They are our kind of people.

***

"You wanted to see me, Doctor G?" Tyrese asked as he came into Livie's office.

"I did. Have a seat. Tyrese, you know better than to wear sunglasses in my classroom. What's going on with you today? You didn't say a word during discussion. Are you okay? You look like you have a headache," Livie said.

"I'm so sorry. I didn't mean to disrespect you, Doctor G. I had a collision with another outfielder last night at baseball practice. We were both going for the ball. I have been really sick on my stomach ever since then, and my eyes just won't focus. The black part of my right eye looks weird. I wore the sunglasses because they made the headache feel better. It won't happen again. I just got my bell rung hard."

"Tyrese, those are the classic symptoms of a concussion," Livie said with alarm. "Pupil dilation is the sign of a serious injury, the kind that can be really dangerous if you don't get medical help."

"The trainer looked at me last night and said I should be fine," Tyrese explained. "She says chances are it's not a concussion. She saw my eye and thought it was probably just because I was tired. We've got a divisional matchup tonight against Arden University that will make or break our playoff hopes. Coach wants me in the starting lineup. If I can get a nap before we have to report to the field tonight, I can handle it. I've played through worse."

"Honey, I want you to call your Mama right now and tell her that you might have a concussion. You need to go home and either be seen by a neurologist or an emergency room today. Where is home for you?"

"Myrtle Beach, SC."

"Okay, you aren't driving. If you can't get a ride, I'll take you. And I'm emailing your coach and the Athletic Director now to tell them that you are not starting tonight."

"Man, coach is going to be pissed at me," Tyrese said, the worry evident in his voice. "This game is everything."

"Tyrese, in the larger scheme of life, this game is absolutely nothing. I am more concerned about your long-term neurological health. And coach is going to be pissed at me, not you, because I'm about to do his job for him."

To: Rialto, Champ; Barnes, Chip
From: Green, Olivia
Sent: Thu 2/17/11 2:11 p.m.

Colleagues,

Tyrese Hammond is enrolled in my Literary Modernism course. In having a discussion with him after class today, it became abundantly clear that he sustained a concussion at last night's baseball practice. Despite the fact that the trainer knew about his nausea, headache, light sensitivity, blurred vision, and enlarged right pupil, she determined that he was cleared to play in tonight's matchup against Arden. I am writing to inform you that Tyrese will not be in the starting lineup. He has been advised to seek medical care through his family's private insurance plan. If you have any questions, please let me know.

Dr. Olivia Green
Associate Professor of English, Clary-Smith University

To: Green, Olivia
From: Rialto, Champ
CC: Barnes, Chip
Sent: Thu 2/17/11 2:20 p.m.

Ms. Green,

I assure you that our athletic training staff is highly skilled and is well aware of the signs of concussion. Their extensive training has prepared them to take the best possible care of our student athletes, who we treat as our own sons and daughters. I will speak to Tyrese if he has concerns about playing in tonight's game.

Champ Rialto
Clary-Smith Athletic Director

To: Rialto, Champ
FROM: Green, Olivia
CC: Barnes, Chip
SENT: Thu 2/17/11 2:24 p.m.

Mr. Rialto,

The athletic trainer who treated Tyrese last night also moonlights at the Taco Bell in Hickory Grove for extra cash. If Tyrese were my son, I wouldn't entrust his enlarged pupil to her medical expertise. Tyrese will not be contacting you about tonight's game. His mother is on her way to campus to pick him up. She and Tyrese are going straight to the emergency room, where he should have gone last night the very minute he was injured.

Dr. Olivia Green
Associate Professor of English, Clary-Smith University

To: Green, Olivia
FROM: Barnes, Chip
CC: Rialto, Champ
SENT: Thu 2/17/11 2:29 p.m.

Ms. Green,

I saw Tyrese this morning at weight training, and he looked fine.

Coach Chip Barnes
Head Baseball Coach, Clary-Smith University

To: Rialto, Champ; Barnes, Chip
From: Green, Olivia
Sent: Thu 2/17/11 9:31 p.m.

Colleagues,

I just heard from Tyrese Hammond's mother. After undergoing an MRI, Tyrese has been admitted to the hospital with a severe concussion. He's not fine. I have been in contact with the university's academics/athletics liaison. I feel certain some additional concussion protocol training is in the cards for your entire staff. The faculty at this institution have historically tolerated a lot of nonsense out of athletics: students missing classes for team meetings, coaches providing little to no notice to students that they will be traveling for away matches, students who are failing classes being allowed to continue with their athletic teams with no intervention from coaches. However, I will not sit silently and watch the physical health of my students be jeopardized in exchange for Division III sports glory. If ever there is another instance of a student's well-being being risked by the irresponsible medical advice of your trainers, you can count on me to speak up about it, and my voice is mighty loud.

Dr. Olivia Green
Associate Professor of English, Clary-Smith University

To: Green, Olivia
FROM: Williams, Callie
SENT: Fri 2/18/11 9:20 a.m.

Dr. Green,

Have you made a decision about whether or not we will have class next Monday considering the winter storm will hit the next day? My Daddy won't let me drive in the ice and snow, and I am already freaking out. My anxiety is so high right now.

Callie Williams
Clary-Smith Class of 2014

To: Williams, Callie
FROM: Green, Olivia
SENT: Fri 2/18/21 9:31 a.m.

Callie,

We are days away from any flakes falling, so take a deep breath. It is unlikely that our class will be canceled the day before the storm as the roads will be just fine then. I will keep you posted if anything changes between now and then.

Dr. Olivia Green
Associate Professor of English, Clary-Smith University

CARTER

I'm at the store with the parents.
Mama wants to know if you have
your bread and milk yet. Daddy
wants to know if you have enough
cement blocks to put in your trunk
in case you have to drive in the
snow next week.

LIVIE

Yes to Daddy on the cement
blocks. And tell Mama I don't really
like milk sandwiches, so I'm good.

CARTER

She says you better not sass your
Mama, especially not with a winter
weather event bearing down on us all.

***

"Tyrese was in my office for counseling today. He told me what you did for him. Thank you for loving them the way we are supposed to love them," said Fitz, passing a newly lit Cuban cigar to Livie. It was so cold on the chapel roof, but they both needed an outdoor break in the worst way.

"How in the world can someone see an injury that severe and not recommend a hospital visit? Just how?" Livie asked.

"You are clearly wired the way I am," Fitz agreed. "I don't know either."

"This place. Some days I don't know how we keep putting one foot in front of the other. How are we supposed to persist? And don't give me any of that 'bloom where you are planted' bullshit," Livie said.

"Oh, good Lord no. I grapple with the same feeling. It's just that there are a lot of people at this university who have been in the echo chamber too long, smelling each other's farts. Sometimes they need us to knock on the door and say, 'Hey, dumbasses, it smells bad in there.' That's what Tyrese needed from you, for you to call out his coaches and trainers. His mom is so glad you stepped in. Thank you for being you."

"And thank you for being you. And for cursing, because you know how happy it makes me on the occasions when you do it."

To: AllFaculty; AllStaff
From: Harper, Denny
Sent: Mon 2/21/11 8:05 a.m.

Dear Colleagues,

The National Weather Service forecast has settled on one inch of snow for our area starting tonight at midnight. Please use caution if you have to travel on the highways as a coating of snow might be possible. The university will issue an Emergency Alert Bulletin in the morning with more information about closings or delays. Stay safe.

Denny Harper
Human Resources Director, Clary-Smith University

February 21, 2011

Clary-Smith Clarion
A Covert Faculty NEWSPAPER

Because higher education is a dumpster fire, and we don't have the budget to buy extinguishers

Dear Colleagues Edition

Dear Coach Barnes, the faculty doesn't need an extra reminder that you have scheduled a damned baseball game at noon on a Tuesday. Blaring music through the scoreboard's loudspeaker during warm-ups while we try to teach the classes your athletes are missing is not well received, so stop it.

Dear Dr. Ponsonby, thank you for taking the opportunity at the last Faculty Assembly to ask President McShitface why he is killing the Humanities.

Dear Dr. Kilpatrick, please cease and desist with the emails about your kid's school fundraiser. Nobody is going to pay $14.95 for 25 square feet of cheap-ass wrapping paper.

Dear Dr. Holland, the microwavable dinner you heat up in the faculty lounge every day at precisely 12:10 p.m. makes the room smell like a sack full of farts for the rest of the day.

Dear Dr. Chu, we all see you riding below the speed limit in the left lane on Highway 415 in the mornings. The left lane is for passing—it's not for hanging out and contemplating the meaning of the universe.

Dear Dr. Goldwell, it's all right to be a militant feminist. What's not all right is berating a newly engaged female student for giving in to the patriarchy or making all of your women's studies classes read nothing but books about women killing men and putting them through woodchippers.

Dear Dr. Pendleton, please stop posting "Unspoken prayer request. God knows the need" on Facebook. If the Almighty is on top of it, you don't need us for anything other than attention.

Dear Champ Rialto, Clary-Smith is a Division III school. That's basically glorified intramurals. Mandatory team meetings will never trump academic classes. Also, stop cheating on your wife with our Finance Director.

CLARY-SMITH UNIVERSITY
EMERGENCY ALERT BULLETIN

TUESDAY, FEBRUARY 22, 2011 4:46 A.M.
University Operating on a One-Hour Delay

While our campus ended up on the rain side of the rain/snow line with the winter storm, the university will still operate on a one-hour delay today (February 22nd) out of an abundance of caution. There is a small chance of an icy glaze on some bridges and overpasses in neighboring counties.

***

"Thanks for stopping by my office, Marshall. Please have a seat wherever you are comfortable," Livie said as she put away her stack of papers and her grade book.

"Am I in trouble, Doctor G.?" Marshall asked hesitantly.

"Oh, no. I just wanted to check in with you because you have seemed a little bit off lately. You haven't been participating in class like you normally do, and you have missed two homework assignments in a row. What's up?"

Marshall sat silently for a long time and twisted his watch, clearly stalling for time as he tried to figure out what to say.

"The thing is," he said and then paused. "The thing is I don't know what to do about my major. Or my parents. I am pre-med and destined for dentistry school. Except I failed my biology course last fall. And I don't mean I just missed the line. I failed the hell out of it. Chemistry this semester isn't going any better. I got a 16/100 on my first chemistry test last week. My parents don't know about the test yet, and they are going to flip out when they do. With another bad semester of science grades, I will not get into dentistry school, and I have to."

"Tell me about that last part—having to get into dentistry school," Livie said.

"Well, my dad is a dentist and my two older brothers are dentists in practice with him. My grandfather was a dentist, and his father was too. So, I am going to be a dentist," he explained with absolutely no expression in his voice.

"Hey, Marshall. Do you care anything about teeth?" Livie asked.

Marshall paused again, but there was no watch spinning this time. Instead, Livie could see his wheels turning. He let them spin for a good minute before responding.

"I don't give a damn about teeth, Doctor G. I've never said that out loud, but it's true. I don't want to be a dentist. The idea of putting my hands in other people's mouths grosses me out. I'm not really sure what I do want to be, but I know it's not a dentist. What am I going to do?"

"Well, you are going to start by allowing yourself to accept that truth. It is okay to have an opinion about what you are going to do with the rest of your life. At some point you will need to tell your family how you really feel, but I think you need to get comfortable with it yourself first. I support you, and I will be glad to help you look through the university's course offerings to find some electives that will allow you to explore new fields in search of a major."

Livie could see tears welling up in Marshall's eyes, though he controlled them enough and kept them from falling. She knew his life had likely included a lot of holding it together to keep from buckling under the pressure.

"I … I appreciate this so much, Doctor G. I can't thank you enough," Marshall said.

"Sweetie, the undergraduate experience at a private liberal arts college should be about exploring. I don't want you to be trapped on a path that you didn't pick. I have always been of the opinion that you have to make your own fun because the world won't do it for you. Take some time to reimagine what your future could be like. This is the most exciting time of your life because you can literally shape it into anything you want it to be. Have some fun considering the possibilities. And get your behind in gear with those homework assignments because we have to repair your GPA after those science tests!"

As Marshall took his bookbag and headed out into the hallway, Livie knew it was only a matter of time before his mom contacted her in a tizzy. Livie also knew not to care too much about that. At this point in her career, she could scope out a helicopter parent a mile away, and her marksmanship was impressive these days.

To: Green, Olivia
From: Thornburg, Kaycee
Sent: Mon 2/28/11 1:54 a.m.

Doctor Green,

You had no right to fail my final rhetorical analysis. Your grading system is just wrong, and you are a bitch.

Kaycee

To: Thornburg, Kaycee
Cc: Godwin, Harris
From: Green, Olivia
Sent: Mon 2/28/11 7:49 a.m.

Kaycee,

Your rhetorical analysis failed because it was supposed to be a five-page essay. You submitted a paragraph of five sentences. That explanation was provided to you with the grade.

You have some good options here, however.

First, since you are so consistently unhappy, you can withdraw from my course. The deadline is next week, so hop to it if that is what you want.

Secondly, you can challenge any grade I give you by filing an appeal with the Honor Board. I would be delighted to take these matters there for resolution.

Finally, you are not allowed to verbally abuse a faculty member. You are in violation of the Student Handbook's Code of Conduct. I have copied the Dean of Students, and you should expect a meeting invitation from him soon to discuss this situation. You will not be allowed back in my classroom until you understand how to respect the academic space.

Dr. Olivia Green
Associate Professor of English, Clary-Smith University

MARCH

March 2, 2011

Clary-Smith Clarion

A Covert Faculty NEWSPAPER

Because higher education is a dumpster fire, and we don't have the budget to buy extinguishers

On Monday, Facilities Manager Frank Abbott was observed inspecting all buildings on campus for violations of the university's policy on moving chairs in classrooms. The Association of Christian Athletes learned the hard way a few months ago that if you move the chairs into a circle for prayer, you better put them back in rows before you leave— or else. Abbott is out for blood.

Dr. Burris has lately, during her unattended office hours, taken to watching YouTube video compilations of people falling down. She finds it is a satisfying metaphor for her work life, and it makes her feel not so alone. According to Burris, "It takes a few years of working here to become a locus of trauma, but once you do, you need to see people falling down to cope."

A burst water pipe on the third floor of the Tavernier dorm Thursday night created the perfect opportunity for residents of the first floor to set up a slip-and-slide in the east wing hallway.

Education professor Dr. Tracy Goins saw Dr. Livie Green put a handful of salty peanuts into her cola at a recent faculty meeting and nearly ralphed. Our guess is that Goins never had the chance to string beans on her Pepaw's porch either.

Faculty and staff who park in Lot B will note that history professor Julie Clayton has taken to parking her prized Mazda Miata backwards in the parking space on Fridays in order to make her 5:00 exit as quickly as possible. Her students might call her "Satan Clayton" behind her back, but she is one of the best teachers this institution has ever employed. If high expectations make you the devil, then so be it.

Eighty-five-pound Education Professor Dr. Alanna Woodhouse is a Muay Thai master. If the shit ever hit the fan in a real way, we would absolutely call her before the Clary-Smith Police Department.

ROGER
I just got this email from a student who was supposed to submit his op-ed draft today. "My draft is not written, but I had to submit something, so...TA-DAH!"

GEORGIANA
Hahaha! Well, there has to be a tiny bit of credit given for submitting something and providing a laugh.

To: AllFaculty; AllStaff
From: Forsythe, Keesha
Sent: Thu 3/3/11 9:13 a.m.

Spring Break is upon us, and this is a great time to begin thinking about your sunscreen protection in the warm months ahead.

Did you know that you can still get a skin-damaging sunburn on a completely overcast day? Did you know that just one sunburn can increase your cancer risk?

The American Academy of Dermatology recommends that anyone outside wear SPF of at least 30 and apply the sunscreen liberally on all exposed skin.

As you hit the beaches this Spring Break, don't forget to pack your sunscreen!

To Good Health,
Keesha Forsythe, RN
Clary-Smith School Nurse

March 7, 2011

Clary-Smith Clarion
A Covert Faculty NEWSPAPER

Because higher education is a dumpster fire, and we don't have the budget to buy extinguishers

School Nurse Keesha Forsythe's health reminder focused this week on sunscreen, something faculty who are in the throes of midterm grading don't exactly have time to fully ponder right now. And considering our salaries, chances are that very few of us will be hitting the beaches over Spring Break. Clarion staff members hear from sources in the athletics department that most athletic teams plan to hold practice over Spring Break, so a large percentage of Clary-Smith's students won't go anywhere and may not even get the opportunity to rest. "The whole point of the break," said English Professor Roger Eumenides, "is for students to get the opportunity to catch up on sleep, visit their families, and blow off some steam. It's pretty shitty that sports are taking that from them." That said, it's good to know that if and when we do all make it to the coast, we need to have some SPF 30 with us.

Speaking of salaries, this week faculty got their first look at the Master's of Science in Nursing curricular proposal and preliminary budget, and it's clear that the new faculty in that program will have no financial concerns about traveling over Spring Break once they are hired. When several faculty pointed out that the senior faculty in the program would have salaries higher than the president, the Dean of Health Sciences, Dr. Henrietta Davenport, explained that these salaries were mandated by the Nursing program's accrediting body. Not satisfied with that answer, one faculty member asked what cuts in other areas would have to be made to accommodate such an exorbitant pay scale. Davenport retorted, "Honestly, it's not like they are making the salaries of NFL players. This is their market value." Boy, we all need to get one of those discipline-specific accrediting bodies to make demands for us.

It has not gone unnoticed that Finance Director Karen Reynolds, who continues to just be a wretched woman, has taken to wearing risqué camisoles underneath the jackets of her pantsuits. Suffice it to say that the fine china could fall out of the cabinet at any moment. An unnamed secretary in the administration building overheard Athletics Director Champ Rialto telling her last Friday that she was "hotter than redneck ass on chili night." When reached for comment about Rialto's statement, English professor Dr. Meryl Kaiser said, "Ew. Barf."

Dr. Lauren Turner is not handling the death of her beloved cat, Bacon, very well. After cuddling with Bacon for the night following his death, her fiancé managed to convince her to bury the animal in the morning. Shortly after he went to work, however, she dug up the cat and took him to a crematorium. Y'all pray for her. Seriously.

To: Green, Olivia
From: Thornburg, Kaycee
Sent: Mon 3/7/11 9:32 a.m.

THIS IS KAYCEE THORNBURGS MOM

I am not gonna let you fail her you are too hard on these kids. They are here just trying to learn and you have to be so hard on them. I already had a talk with the Prevost this morning and we are gonna take care of this. You just wait and see. You are gonna be sorry you every decided to pick on my baby. She is going to be a lawyer and take down people LIKE YOU. I can't believe you still have a job here but we will be handling that too You better watch your back.

To: Thornburg, Kaycee
CC: Godwin, Harris
From: Green, Olivia
Sent: Mon 3/7/11 9:40 a.m.

Kaycee,

It appears as though your mother used your Clary-Smith email account to send me a message. Remember that FERPA regulations prevent me from talking about your performance in the class with anyone other than you. As well, allowing anyone other than yourself to use your university-issued email address is a violation of the Student Handbook.

Dr. Olivia Green
Associate Professor of English, Clary-Smith University

To: AllFaculty
From: Godwin, Harris
Sent: Mon 3/7/11 4:49 p.m.
Subject: Student Trespassed from Campus

Faculty and Staff,

Freshman student Kaycee Thornburg has been trespassed from campus. She is no longer allowed to be on university property. If you see her or her vehicle (white Kia four-door sedan NC plates HYF-6744) please notify Clary-Smith Police Officer Boyce Lowder immediately.

Harris Godwin, Dean of Students
Clary-Smith University

LIVIE
Bad day at work. Make me
smile somehow.

CARTER
Well Mama is probably moving in with you.
This morning when she went to wash a load
of towels, she discovered a six-foot-long black
snake coiled up in her laundry basket. She's
refusing to come back in the house even
though Daddy told her he killed it. The
truth is it slithered under the dryer, and he
doesn't know where the damn thing is.
Anyway, the preacher is over here praying
with Mama on the front porch as I type.

LIVIE
No bueno.

To: Green, Olivia
From: Alder, Dutch
Sent: Wed 3/9/11 7:36 a.m.

Hey, Livie. Just a heads up, and I hope it will catch you before you walk face-first into the administrative weed eaters this morning. The Advancement office is entertaining Eustis and Birdie Bettencourt. Eustis is a Business program alum, and the Advancement staff is falling all over themselves trying to secure his donation. They are talking about millions of dollars for the Bettencourt School of Business building on the east side of campus. But here's the kicker. Birdie is apparently bored out of her gourd and needs a distraction. The Bettencourts are angling for Birdie's hire as a Creative Writing professor in the English department. She thinks she's a poet and wants to take over our literary magazine as the editor-in-chief. She has a B.S. in Counseling from 1967. If this deal goes through, the Bettencourts will usurp Meryl Kaiser's whole job, and the university will probably fire her. You have to do something, and you better think fast. I hear Birdie and Eustis will be on campus today with their checkbook.

Dr. Dutch Alder
Clary-Smith Art Department (All of It—It's Just Me)

To: Green, Olivia
From: Grim, Ronald
Sent: Wed 3/9/11 10:04 a.m.

Dr. Green,

As the program coordinator of the English program, I need you to join me this afternoon at 3:00 in the Advancement office for a meeting with potential donors Eustis and Birdie Bettencourt. Please bring a copy of the latest edition of *The Beacon* so we can showcase our wonderful literary magazine.

Dr. Ronald Grim
Dean of Humanities and Sciences, Clary-Smith University

To: Grim, Ronald
From: Green, Olivia
Sent: Wed 3/9/11 10:06 a.m.

Dr. Grim,

I teach at 3:00, and my students are giving graded oral presentations, so I can't have another professor cover. As well, I am aware that the Bettencourts are interested in making a donation to Clary-Smith only if Mrs. Bettencourt is hired by my program as a creative writing professor and given full control of the literary magazine. We already have a creative writing professor with a Ph.D. and 10 years of experience leading award-winning campus literary magazines in Dr. Meryl Kaiser. Our literary magazine is run by a student editorial board. It is not faculty controlled. Please tell the Bettencourts that we appreciate their interest in our program, but it is not for sale.

Dr. Olivia Green
Associate Professor of English, Clary-Smith University

To: Green, Olivia
From: Grim, Ronald
Sent: Wed 3/9/11 11:15 a.m.

Dr. Green,

You will cancel your 3:00 class and meet me in the Advancement conference room. As the program coordinator, you do not control hiring within the program. Those decisions are above your pay grade. You will bring the copy of the literary magazine as requested.

Dr. Ronald Grim
Dean of Humanities and Sciences, Clary-Smith University

To: Grim, Ronald
From: Green, Olivia
Sent: Wed 3/9/11 11:23 a.m.

Dr. Grim,

You are correct that this administration will not allow faculty enough autonomy to make the best decisions for the students in their programs. Where you are wrong is in thinking faculty are going to stand by and allow you to auction academic programs off to the highest bidder. I had a fascinating conversation this morning with our SCRAMPI faculty liaison, Dr. Samantha Carey. After doing some research, I learned that the faculty body at every SCRAMPI-accredited school is assigned an impartial intermediary who can help them advocate for themselves when the administration is making decisions that go against SCRAMPI standards and who can offer protection for faculty who are afraid of retaliation for blowing the whistle. It turns out that

SCRAMPI standard 5.3.7 prohibits the university from hiring an un-credentialed faculty member to teach a credit-bearing course. You will remember that last year the English program converted *The Beacon* from an activity to a credit-bearing course for a grade. Do you still need me to cancel my class and bring the magazine at 3:00 or are we good?

Dr. Olivia Green
Associate Professor of English, Clary-Smith University

March 11, 2011

Clary-Smith Clarion
A Covert Faculty NEWSPAPER

Because higher education is a dumpster fire, and we don't have the budget to buy extinguishers

Bettencourts Land at Clary-Smith

Eustis and Birdie Bettencourt have inked a deal with the Advancement office to donate $10 million for the Bettencourt School of Business. The negotiations will also bring Mrs. Bettencourt to campus full-time as the editor of the student newspaper. If that sounds funny to you, don't feel bad. Students should actually run the student newspaper, but the administration agreed to the deal only after a quick-thinking Dr. Olivia Green spared the English department from the Bettencourt's plan to bring Mrs. Bettencourt onto the faculty as a creative writing professor and head of *The Beacon*, the university's literary magazine. Dr. Green outsmarted the world's worst dean in her discovery of SCRAMPI faculty liaison Dr. Samantha Carey, who made it clear that Bettencourt did not have the education to be credentialed and essentially steal Dr. Meryl Kaiser's job. Thankfully for the English program, their out with *The Beacon* was that they transitioned it to a credit-bearing course through the Curriculum Board last year, thus making it a course that had to be credentialed. Unfortunately for the Communications faculty, the same couldn't be said for the campus newspaper. In the wake of the news, the entire student newspaper staff has already quit. Dr. Green is on the agenda at next week's Faculty Senate meeting to explain to the entire faculty how a relationship with the faculty liaison can be fully maximized.

MERYL
Thank you. Thank you for not
telling me and just doing what
you had to do.

LIVIE
You'd do the same for me if roles were
reversed. There's no way I would let
that rich old bag take your job. You
are magnificent at what you do.

To: Patterson, Felicitie
From: Green, Olivia
Sent: Mon 3/21/11 9:32 a.m.

Felicitie,

I just graded your annotated bibliography, and you earned a B-. I wanted to email you to recognize how hard you worked on that assignment. You pushed through, even though you were struggling and frustrated. You also never stopped working, and you took my advice about visiting the Writing Center. All of that wasn't easy with your basketball practice and game schedule either. I am proud of you.

Dr. Olivia Green
Associate Professor of English, Clary-Smith University

To: Green, Olivia
From: Patterson, Felicitie
Sent: Mon 3/21/11 11:01 a.m.

Dr. G,

I saw the grade a few minutes ago and emailed your comments to my Auntie. She's already got it up on the fridge. I would have never thought I could get a B on a college paper. I'm so excited.

Felicitie

***

"So tell me about the Camp Wish Makers Spring Break trip," Livie said as she scooted the rooftop chaise lounge into the sunshine. "All of the students who came back are just raving about it. They can't wait to go back and serve."

"It was truly one of the most profound experiences of my life," Fitz said, as he tried to decide which new cigar to try first. "This university absolutely drains me. Weeks like that revive my spirit and give me the strength to keep moving. To see our students pouring themselves into the lives of chronically ill children and doing everything they could to make sure they had a good time was just …" His voice cut out as he fought to handle the emotion. "It was life-changing—for all of us."

"I'm coming next time," Livie said, liking the flavor of the cigar he chose. "Go ahead and put me on the list."

"Meanwhile, in Cancun," Fitz said with a devious grin forming, "Tripp McLovelace and three other lacrosse players used their spring break to get themselves arrested for stealing a keg of beer off the beach of a neighboring resort. And get this: beer was completely free at their own resort. There is just nothing quite like a night in Mexican jail, I've heard."

"Where did you hear that?" Livie asked, sitting straight up in her chair.

"Oh, it's fact," Fitz confirmed. "The president had to cancel a board meeting at the very last minute and hop a plane with the university's lawyer to bail them all out."

March 22, 2011

Clary-Smith Clarion
A Covert Faculty NEWSPAPER

Because higher education is a dumpster fire, and we don't have the budget to buy extinguishers

Reverend Fitzgerald Duval's week-long service trip to Camp Wish Makers in Orlando, Florida, was absolutely transformational for the 14 students, 5 staff, and 2 faculty who participated. Camp Wish Makers provides all-expenses-paid vacations for chronically and terminally ill children and their families at facilities that are manned by medical professionals and equipped with the technology to make the trips possible. All Clary-Smith participants had to pay their own trip expenses with no subsidy from the university, but those who went on the trip would have paid double considering all they got out of the experience. It was the most impactful university-sanctioned event of the academic year. In fact, several students came back from the trip with new a career direction and a new passion for service.

And in other good news, the outcry against the administration's push to have the 11:00 chapel hour removed was so effective that the proposal has been tabled while the administration tries to figure out how to do the right thing for a change.

The Clarion staff has learned that a new dean will be joining the team. Over the summer, the university plans to hire a Dean of Innovation. One would think that the 20 deans we have would already be innovating on a pretty large scale. The new Dean of Innovation will be housed in the Public Relations office. At this point, our organizational chart looks like a Mr. Potato Head built by a preschooler—you know, with the feet on the ass and two eyeballs for shoes.

Crazy Bill is now exercising on the Clary-Smith walking trail in the evenings. While he can't verbally condemn you to the eternal fire while you pass by, he sure can shake his Bible at you, and you should know that he absolutely will.

Institutional Research Director Dr. Gladys Myers recently called maintenance to her office for help with fixing her table lamp. Brent and Lester arrived as a team to assist, but it only took Lester to figure out that the lamp wasn't plugged in.

To: AllFaculty; AllStaff
From: McLovelace, Grady
Sent: Wed 3/24/11 10:21 a.m.

All faculty and staff should be advised that the Clary-Smith
administration will no longer tolerate the publication of the
"Clarion," the so-called faculty newspaper. Be advised that any
employee at Clary-Smith who is caught with a copy of the Clarion
will have a report documented in their permanent HR behavior
and comportment files. We will find out who is publishing this
nonsense, and there will be consequences.

Dr. Grady McLovelace
President, Clary-Smith University

March 25, 2011

Clary-Smith Clarion
A Covert Faculty NEWSPAPER

Because higher education is a dumpster fire, and we don't have the budget to buy extinguishers

President Shady McShitface's recent threat against faculty for reading the Clarion has created a firestorm the administration did not anticipate. Faculty and staff members all over campus have begun taping Clarion editions to their office doors in defiance of the president's decree. Meanwhile, Crazy Bill, a rabid fan of the First Amendment if there ever was one, has voiced his support of the faculty's right to publish whatever they want from his perch on the stone wall in the Free Speech Zone. Human Resources Administrative Assistant Cody Jackson confirms that there is no such thing as a "permanent HR behavior and comportment file." The truth is that a server crash a few years ago wiped out almost all the personal data of employees hired before 2008. Most of them don't have any kind of file at all. Nice bluff, Grady.

If you didn't come to the community band's spring concert, you really missed out. The ensemble is made up of Clary-Smith music majors and any other community members who want to participate, no matter where their skill levels are. English professor Dr. Meryl Kaiser has played the clarinet with the band for several years now, and the students absolutely LOVE having her play an instrument with them. It's such a beautiful way to teach them about interdisciplinarity. This year's concert did have one small hiccup. During the Spanish "Malagueña," the fairly inexperienced trumpet line got off the beat, and Music professor Dr. Brian McNary had to stop the ensemble in the middle of the song to start over. A percussionist who was required on beats two and four of every measure to crash the hell out of the cymbals couldn't even hear that the rest of the band had stopped, and someone had to walk over and tap her on the shoulder.

We have clearly reached the point in the program where someone needs to intervene with Finance Director Karen Reynolds. She showed up to the Board of Trustees meeting in an outfit that consisted of a whole set of questionable decisions. The top part of the ensemble turned out to be the pressing issue, as one of her very stressed top buttons gave way, creating a show and tell that nobody wanted to see.

The library staff report that sometimes the English majors use the slang dictionaries in the reference room to look up the etymologies of bad words. Sometimes the English faculty do too.

TAMMY JANE
I have a confession to make.

LIVIE
Spill Jill.

TAMMY JANE
For the past few years on my lunch breaks, I have been using Grim's university email address to sign him up for every marketing/spam opportunity I can find–sometimes dozens every day.

LIVIE
HAHAHAHAHAHAHAHAHAHAHAHA!

TAMMY JANE
I do it so his inbox stays full. He is more tolerable when I can keep him occupied with work for an hour here and there.

LIVIE
As a sign of solidarity, I will start doing the same thing. This is pure genius.

March 28, 2011

Clary-Smith Clarion
A Covert Faculty NEWSPAPER

Because higher education is a dumpster fire, and we don't have the budget to buy extinguishers

McShitface Gets Wasted at Athletic Honors Banquet

Saturday's 24th Annual Athletics Honors Banquet was marked by the usual dick-measuring showmanship of such events, as fifteen student athletes were celebrated for their ability to run and hit balls with sticks. The highlight of the night, however, was President McShitface living up to his nickname at the cash bar. Sources who were in attendance tell us that his penchant for Long Island iced teas got the best of him once again. The Athletic Director should have known better than to put the president's speech at the end of the night, when he is much more likely to slur his words and get handsy with the women's volleyball players. The ogre is a Title IX grievance just waiting for somewhere to happen. Also noteworthy was the fact that the athletic prowess of the university's students was celebrated with an ice sculpture of a squirrel kicking a soccer ball. Yay sports.

MERYL
Alert! Alert! Alert! Jazzmyn
Sykes got into graduate school!

LIVIE
YES! She worked so hard.

ROGER
That's incredible. Way to go, Jazz.

GEORGIANA
I couldn't be any more proud of
her if she was my very own child.

LIVIE
Please don't tell the dean.
You know what will happen.

DENISE
What will happen? Though I
am truly scared to ask.

LIVIE
The Marketing department will show up
unannounced at her dorm with a camera
crew asking her invasive questions about
how Clary-Smith helped her succeed as
an African American student for their
next promotional piece. I can see the
insulting headline now: "From the Ghetto
to Graduate School."

GEORGIANA
I hope to God they don't find out she's
gay. They're always on the prowl for
minorities to exploit on the cover of the
latest edition of the alumni magazine.
Black AND homosexual would be like
the diversity jackpot for them.

MERYL
You remember last year they were
frothing at the mouth over that Native
American freshman student who was
also a female active-duty National Guard

member. Her mom eventually had to call
the Advancement office and tell them to
leave her daughter alone. They wanted
her to pose in her uniform in front of the
flagpole. And they actually asked her if
she had a headdress.

ROGER
Is that why we had to do
that online cultural sensitivity
training module for HR?

LIVIE
Indeed it is.

March 30, 2011

Clary-Smith Clarion
A Covert Faculty NEWSPAPER

Because higher education is a dumpster fire, and we don't have the budget to buy extinguishers

Sports Balls Ruin $2,800 Worth of Visiting Artist's Canvases

Those on campus who actually value the liberal arts were saddened to hear of the fate of the long-awaited acrylic-on-canvas show of nationally renowned visiting artist Leticia Guttierez. After months of unsuccessful negotiation with departments all over campus to secure an appropriate gallery space for the gala, Professor Dutch Alder settled for the visual and acoustic cesspool that is the Byron O. Keith gymnasium.

Unfortunately for critical thought in general and for Leticia Guttierez in particular, the Clary-Smith Flying Squirrel Men's Basketball team made the Division III playoffs in surprise fashion. Without informing anyone, head coach Tony Spry held an impromptu lunchtime practice a mere six hours before the opening reception and roughly sixteen hours after Guttierez's series of 10 oversized canvases had been installed. One canvas was completely destroyed by errant shots, and several others were heavily damaged.

With only hours to work and literally nowhere else available to display the remaining unscathed four canvases, Alder drove into Hickory Grove, rented a box truck, and hung the pieces in the back. Alder's only comment was that it "was no big deal. These athletes will remember this epic hoops season for the rest of their lives when they are basketball coaches in rural middle schools all over the Southeast."

DENISE
You guys, I just saw McJuicington
break red on the vending machine
downstairs. It kept his quarter after
he bought an apple juice. His anger
was uncontained, and I was a little
bit scared. One of my students came
to me for help.

GEORGIANA
You should see it when the
machine takes his money
altogether. It happened last
year just outside my freshman
composition class. He just
melted down.

ROGER
How much liquid does this man consume in a day?

March 31, 2011

Clary-Smith Clarion
A Covert Faculty NEWSPAPER

Because higher education is a dumpster fire, and we don't have the budget to buy extinguishers

The Diversity and Inclusivity Committee has filed a grievance with the Campus Events Board in regard to Professor Dutch Alder's last-minute venue change for the Leticia Guttierez art gala to the back of a handicapped-inaccessible rental van. Filed on behalf of sixth-year senior Dakota McFarland, the co-captain of the lacrosse team who has still not completed his campus events graduation requirement, the grievance alleges that the student was barred from participating in the art gala and thus unable to get his attendance card approved because he is on crutches due a torn ACL and couldn't climb up in the back of the truck.

The Clary-Smith Counseling Center continues its years-long skid, as multiple students have reported that lead counselor Garvin Harbeson has told them in sessions that "most college students don't need counselors because homesick isn't a medical diagnosis." He also told a sexual assault survivor that it was "time that she just got over it." Garvin's genius has extended to the development of the new peer counseling program that will afford his lazy ass the opportunity to see even fewer students each week. Untrained and unskilled federal Work Study students are now being deployed to meet with prospective Counseling Center clients to see if they can handle them first. One of Dr. Beth Hollins's music majors is participating in the program and explained, "Garvin just gave us these tie-dyed 'Peer Counselors Rock' T-shirts and told us to go try to help students. I really don't know what I'm supposed to do, so most of the time I just help the clients with their homework." No doubt, Garvin will be praised by the administration for his "focus on creating a sustainable program model."

Dr. Georgiana Ponsonby's most recent brilliant idea is the formation of a grassroots faculty group dedicated to helping colleagues set publishing goals and follow through with them. The group's popularity increases each month, and several faculty members have already produced articles that are sure to be accepted to peer-reviewed journals. Note to the administration: this is what works—organic unforced bottom-up leadership. Leave us alone, give us just a minute, and we can create something meaningful.

Meanwhile in the cafeteria, Dr. Wyatt Hayden from the Psychology department continues to slow down the salad bar line at the peak of the lunch rush. I mean get a grip and make a choice, man.

She's okay, so don't worry, but Georgiana Ponsonby was injured yesterday in her British Literature class while standing on a chair and trying to insert a DVD of *Pride and Prejudice* into the machine mounted below the television. After misjudging the height of the DVD player, she clocked the back side of her head with some force. Students reported that she said "fuck" real loud before she blacked out.

APRIL

DENISE
I need help with this one. Today in my
freshman composition course, one of my
students let a toot. It was loud, and right
afterward she said, "My bad. Couldn't hold it."

MERYL
Hmm. While it is a natural body function,
you shouldn't do that in public out of
respect for those around you.

DENISE
It took a few seconds to come on,
but man it was potent.

LIVIE
That's not okay. The American college
classroom is disrespected enough these
days with students wearing earbuds and
trying to sleep in the back row. I draw the
line at openly farting. I would have told
her that passing gas is not appropriate
for a business setting, so she should be
practicing respectful behaviors now to
prepare herself for the world of work.

GEORGIANA
I'm torn here. I'm just happy when
they show up to class having actually
completed the reading. I don't care
about booty bombs as long as they have
something coherent to say about the text.

ROGER
Maybe we should pose this topic as a
roundtable discussion for the next professional
development brown bag. It would be more
interesting than another advising tutorial.

MERYL
If I have to sit through another session where
the Dean of Advising breaks out that same
presentation I'm going to flip a desk.

April 1, 2011

Clary-Smith Clarion

A Covert Faculty NEWSPAPER

Because higher education is a dumpster fire, and we don't have the budget to buy extinguishers

BREAKING NEWS: Rialto, Reynolds Caught in Trailblazer Tryst (No, this is not an April Fools joke)

Athletic Director Champ Rialto and Finance Director Karen Reynolds were caught in the throes of passion at dusk last night by two very generous alumni donors who were out for a twilight stroll on the Clary-Smith walking trail. The alumni saw Rialto's Chevy Trailblazer, which was parked beside Troy Lake, shaking with such force that they feared someone was having a medical emergency inside. Thank God Crazy Bill isn't the one who made the discovery. Public fornication right before his very eyes may very well have caused him to spontaneously combust with judgment. This is an evolving scandal with wide-reaching implications, so stay tuned to the Clarion for more details.

To: AllFaculty; AllStaff
From: Forsythe, Keesha
Sent: Fri 4/1/11 8:10 a.m.

This month's preventative health tip relates to productivity: how you increase your efficiency at work. Below are some suggestions that can help you make the most of your work time so that you go home each day feeling like you have done your best and accomplished your goals.

1. Avoid "time suck" activities like viewing social media or playing online games.

2. Periodically take a break and move around to jumpstart your thinking—maybe take a stroll outside to clear your head.

3. Track your time to know exactly how you are spending it. If you spent a whole morning making corrections to your expense reports, you may need to find a way to reallocate time in order to prevent making so many mistakes on the reports in the first place.

4. Prioritize your tasks so that the most important items on your to-do list get completed first. Handle the deadline before the project that you can complete on your own time.

5. Incorporate healthy snacks into your daily work routine to balance your blood sugar—maybe a handful of almonds or an apple.

6. Choose your meeting schedule carefully. Did you know that the American worker spends an average of 29 hours per month in meetings they gain no value from? Just imagine what you could do with that lost time!

7.   Regularly update your technology to make sure it is making your work space more efficient and not less so.

8.   Map your office/departmental processes to see where wasted effort can be eliminated. You may find that many of the things you invest time in are really not needed at all.

To Good Health,
Keesha Forsythe, RN
Clary-Smith School Nurse

April 2, 2011

Clary-Smith Clarion
A Covert Faculty NEWSPAPER

Because higher education is a dumpster fire, and we don't have the budget to buy extinguishers

In case the email got lost in your inbox, this week school nurse Keesha Forsythe sent some very helpful tips about workplace productivity that you should check out.

1. Avoid time "time suck" activities like walking around with a clip board to see if your faculty have posted their office hours on their doors, or sulking because Tammy Jane Hillyer didn't get the colored paperclips that you like—even though she knows how happy they make you.

2. Periodically take a break and move around—maybe stroll up to the lake and see if Champ Rialto is getting a blow job from the Finance Director in the back of his Trailblazer, or walk over to the Admissions office and see if their cotton candy booth is still open.

3. Track your time to know exactly how you are spending it. If you spent the whole morning working a puzzle of New York's Times Square, maybe you could spend the afternoon talking to your colleagues to see what they are doing today.

4. Prioritize your tasks so that the most important items on your to-do list get completed first. Make time to meet with the student who is having trouble finding sources for her research paper in the library, and postpone less meaningful tasks like filling out a request form to choose your own clothing or attending a professional development workshop

about "Dreaming Big for Your Academic Program Even Though We Don't Have Money to Make Any of Those Dreams a Reality."

5. Incorporate healthy snacks into your daily work routine to balance your blood sugar—maybe grab an apple juice from the vending machine and then, when it takes your money, scream at it loudly enough to prompt a shaken bystander to call the counseling center for an emergency mental health response.

6. Choose your meeting schedule carefully. Did you know that the Clary-Smith faculty member spends an average of 29 hours per week in meetings with no value? Just imagine what you could do with that lost time!

7. Regularly update your technology to make sure it is making your work space more efficient and not less so. If you are eventually granted access, make your photocopies in the Health Sciences building because their new copier machines are just spectacularly fast, whereas the mimeograph machine in your building vibrates like a jackhammer for 30 seconds before it spits out a single copy with a loud "oooof" like it has been punched in the gut.

8. Map your academic program's processes to see where wasted effort can be eliminated. You may find that many of your university's deans are really not needed at all.

To: Green, Olivia
From: Gates, Clint
Sent: Mon 4/4/11 11:55 a.m.

Dear Dr. Green,

I got a little bit behind with your class this semester. What do I need to do to catch up? I would like to pull out at least a C in the course.

Clint

To: Gates, Clint
From: Green, Olivia
Sent: Mon 4/4/11 1:32 p.m.

Clint,

You have not attended class or submitted any assignments since January. You were removed from the course roster months ago. Since you are in your email, check it. You will see all of my messages about your course standing.

Dr. Olivia Green
Associate Professor of English, Clary-Smith University

DENISE
I couldn't sleep last night, so I decided around
6:00 a.m. to just come in to work. The two
maintenance workers for our building were in my
office. One was taking a nap on my couch, and the
other was sitting in my chair with his feet up on
my desk eating my jelly beans.

ROGER
Hahahahahahahaha! What did
they do when you walked in?

DENISE
The one at my desk stood up really fast and
walked past me to wake up his buddy. And they
just left.

MERYL
Maybe that is where all my
caramels have been going all
these years. Mystery solved.

ROGER
Are you going to report it?

DENISE
Oh, God no. They probably make $7.25
an hour. If that were me, I'd be looking
for a place to secretly take a nap and
eat somebody else's candy too.

LIVIE
No need to report. Brent and Lester are great.
If you think our dean is bad, you should meet
Frank Abbott, their boss. They truly deserve a
moment to escape.

April 8, 2011

Clary-Smith Clarion
A Covert Faculty NEWSPAPER

Because higher education is a dumpster fire, and we don't have the budget to buy extinguishers

The Unfathomable Waste Files:
Student Affairs Edition

In March, Undergraduate Activities Director Kelly Cantrell used Student Affairs budget money to hire an artist to spend the day in the student union writing student names on grains of rice for free. The artist, coincidentally Cantrell's daughter-in-law, was paid $3,000. These events, according to the Dean of Campus Life, promote community building and create an atmosphere of fun considering the campus's rural location. Having one's name written on a grain of rice apparently makes one feel less isolated out here in the literal middle of nowhere. When reached for comment about this story, art professor Dutch Alder wanted it to be known that the entire annual operating budget for the art program is $975.

Stripper-turned-car-wax-entrepreneur-turned-motivational speaker Kalvin Kosmo was contracted by Student Affairs to speak to the student body this month in the chapel. His presentation, themed "You Can Be Anything You Want to Be," contained more clichés than the English majors could stomach. Students were likewise confused about why he offered his speech without a shirt on. Others were offended that Kosmo's sex worker past was remembered with fondness in the house of the Lord. The audience was also uncomfortably pressured to buy Kosmo's branded car wax as they exited the building. Crazy Bill's protest of the event kept him busy for the better part of the day. When reached for comment about this story, art professor Dutch Alder stared blankly off into the distance.

The Clarion has learned that the worse-than-mediocre coffee and Danish service Student Affairs orders each month from the dining hall catering menu for its student leader meetings comes at a cost of $450. For the roughly twenty people in attendance, that comes out to $22.50 a head. In essence, they could all eat lunch at Chili's and get a margarita for the same cost. When reached for comment about this story, art professor Dutch Alder asked that he not be contacted for future stories. His therapist thinks it's just best that he doesn't know.

To: AllFaculty; AllStaff
From: McLovelace, Grady
Sent: Wed 4/11/11 4:50 p.m.

Colleagues,

I wanted to share with you an exciting new promotion that will launch next week. Our Marketing Department continues to innovate and develop creative ways to draw new students into the Clary-Smith family. Beginning next week, a coupon for 10% off tuition and fees for all new students will be published in every print newspaper in the state. According to T'Wana Jones, the Director of Marketing and Promotions, "the investment of our advertising dollars in print media will expand Clary-Smith's profile in North Carolina and position us for a much more aggressive recruitment plan in the coming year." Well done, Marketing staff. If you see them around campus today, please congratulate them.

Dr. Grady McLovelace
President, Clary-Smith University

LIVIE
We have been discounted like a
pack of almost-expired bologna.

MERYL
Maybe our promotion next
month could be a BOGO:
Buy a Bachelor's degree and
get a Master's for free. Look
at me. I innovated.

ROGER
Are we going to accept
competitor coupons from Duke?
Wait. Is Duke issuing coupons
too?

GEORGIANA
Do you think the administration
knows that the only people
reading print newspapers these
days are the elderly with no
access to the Interwebs?

April 14, 2011

Clary-Smith Clarion
A Covert Faculty NEWSPAPER

Because higher education is a dumpster fire, and we don't have the budget to buy extinguishers

Deferred Maintenance Tidbits

The sliding side door of the campus service center van has fallen off on a service trip once again. This time it happened at 65 miles per hour on west-bound Interstate 40 with twelve students aboard on their way to serve in an Appalachian soup kitchen in Tennessee for the weekend. Junior Graphic Art major Kait-Lynn Newton was napping in the third row, closest to the door when it flew off. The force of the wind gust sucked the pillow right out from under her head. Because the service center does not have the funds to properly repair the door, they had to stop at Walmart and purchase enough bungee cords to rubber-band it to the vehicle. When they stop at a site to do service now, they look like a bunch of clowns bailing out of the front seat of a Volkswagen.

Ongoing chemical imbalances in the swim team's pool due to lack of funding for proper maintenance have resulted in another mystery fungus causing unspeakable rashes on the skin in between the fingers and toes of both the men's and women's teams. School nurse Keesha Forsythe has prescribed a topical cream that she is "85% sure will do the trick." On the bright side, Dr. Javier Arias has turned the unfortunate outbreak into an engaged learning project for his Environmental Science class. The first student team who can figure out the balance of the pool chemicals that will eradicate the fungus will not have to take their final exam.

Installed in 1964, the library's elevator, known among students as "the death trap," continues to get stuck on a weekly basis. The alarm button no longer works, so trapped bibliophiles have to use their feet to kick the door loudly enough for someone working the front desk to hear them. Just use the damn stairs.

LIVIE
After three weeks of emailing and requests
in two in-person meetings, the Dean of
Nothingness finally sent me the English budget
update I know for a fact has been in his
possession for four months.

MERYL
His face just makes me so angry.

GEORGIANA
His salary makes me so angry.

LIVIE
But let's bear in mind
that he doesn't make as
much as those NFL players.

MERYL
So true, Dr. Green.

LIVIE
A wise person once offered me that
perspective, and it was so helpful.
How is the noggin today, Duchess?
Is it healing up from the collision
with the DVD player?

GEORGIANA
I was doing okay until I graded 10 freshman
comp papers in a row this afternoon. They
were infuriating. Nobody is listening in class.

ROGER
Yeah, the multimodal drafts
I have seen so far from
students are so weak.

LIVIE
It is against my religion to schedule meetings late in the semester. You know this. But we probably do need to meet to chart a plan just in case the failure rate is abysmal this semester. We'll need to make curricular changes for the fall. I promise there will be a task list, and I'll make sure every minute is productive.

GEORGIANA
You'd never make it as a Clary-Smith dean, Livie Green. Never in a million years.

April 18, 2011

Clary-Smith Clarion

A Covert Faculty NEWSPAPER

Because higher education is a dumpster fire, and we don't have the budget to buy extinguishers

Catastrophic Diarrhea Strikes International Fair (Moldy Baklava Suspected)

Saturday's 9th Annual International Fair was marred by a significant diarrheal outbreak that sidelined more than half of the participants.

After the festival was forced to close shortly before noon, International Club President Molly Kriegel encouraged any festival-goer with gastric distress to see school nurse Keesha Forsythe immediately.

Several students who were stricken reported that they ate the Greek booth's "sketchy baklava," which some suspected was several weeks old due to its stale flavor. One freshman student who asked to remain nameless due to embarrassment said of the dessert, "Man, it was not good. Not. Good. After what that baklava did to my insides, I'll never trust a fart again."

The Student Union offered sports drinks and bottles of water at no charge all weekend to prevent dehydration among those who were sickened. Professor McJuicington was seen trolling the area with his tote bag.

GEORGIANA
I swear to God, whatever is blooming
out there smells like sperm.

MERYL
And ... I'm done with my yogurt.

Faculty Senate Formal Grievance:

PLAINTIFF: DR. OLIVIA J. GREEN
PROGRAM: ENGLISH
SUPERVISOR: DR. RONALD GRIM
DEFENDANT: DR. RONALD GRIM
DATE: APRIL 19, 2011

Summary: According to the timeline set forth in the Faculty Handbook, Dr. Ronald Grim was required to provide faculty in the Humanities and Sciences with a written evaluation of their job performance during the 2009-2010 academic year no later than July 1, 2010. Dr. Grim did not distribute these evaluations until April 11, 2011, more than nine months late. Dr. Grim gave Dr. Olivia Green the next-to-lowest mark in the "Teaching" category, noting "Dr. Green's classroom pedagogies are outdated, and she needs to give more thought to the design of her teaching." Dr. Green is filing a formal grievance about this evaluation, claiming that Dr. Grim has never once observed her in any classroom, in either a formal or informal context. Despite the fact that the Faculty Handbook states that all deans will observe teaching faculty at least once during the academic year and provide written observation feedback, Dr. Grim has never done so in the three years that he has been her direct supervisor.

Outcome of Grievance: On April 20, 2011, the Senate found in favor of Dr. Green. Dr. Grim was not justified in criticizing Dr. Green's teaching because he has never actually seen her teach. Dr. Grim has until the end of April 2011 to complete a teaching observation for each of his teaching faculty members in order to come into compliance with the Faculty Handbook.

April 22, 2011

Clary-Smith Clarion
A Covert Faculty NEWSPAPER

Because higher education is a dumpster fire, and we don't have the budget to buy extinguishers
Homecoming 2011 Edition

By all accounts from the rational people in attendance, Homecoming Weekend 2011 was a smashing success. However, as expected, the litany of complaints to the Advancement office about this and that commenced on Monday morning. Below is a selection of the concerns that were brought to the attention of organizers.

1. Apparently the Class of '63 is deeply invested in the prospect of high-quality appetizers. The lack of shrimp cocktail at this year's reception was noted with disgust by no fewer than 10 alums from that graduating class.
2. The deejay did not play "The Electric Slide," and the class of '72 had been practicing to be ready.
3. The napkins included in the place settings did not feel substantial. They were cloth instead of paper, but they were not very thick.
4. There were not enough floral decorations. The decorating committee needs to focus on making a bigger impact with the decorations.
5. There were too many floral decorations, and the arrangements on the tables at dinner were too big, making it difficult to talk to the people on the other side.
6. The balloons in the archway used for the photo backdrop were limp.

7. The reserved alumni seating at the Saturday baseball game was too far away from the bathroom.
8. At the dedication of the park bench donated by the Class of '68, several alums complained that the engraved plaque giving them credit for the donation was not large enough to be seen from a distance.

***

"Olivia June, I know I'm not supposed to call your office phone number, but I've been good about it all year," Mama Green said breathless. "You have to give me just this one."

"What is it, Mama? Are you and Daddy okay?" Livie asked, realizing that she would need to text Fitz to let him know the cigar bar would have to be closed today.

"The church elders had a meeting this morning and just made the announcement that the preacher and his wife are getting a divorce. The whole church is just falling apart before my very eyes," Mama said, the anxiety rising in her chest with every word.

"Okay, I need you to pump the brakes and assess the situation here," Livie said, trying to keep Mama from falling apart. "Let's get some perspective. You and Daddy aren't getting a divorce, so this is not our crisis. This is external and removed from us."

"Everybody in town is already talking about it. It's going to be so bad," Mama said, having not calmed down even a smidge. "I don't know what we're going to do. It's just a disaster. When do you get off work? Can you come over here?"

"Of course," Livie said. "I will be there by 5:30."

"Glory and hallelujah. That might be the only thing going right today."

LIVIE
What are you doing tonight?

CARTER
Nope.

LIVIE
What?

CARTER
Not doing it. I heard about the D-I-V-O-R-C-E in line at the BBQ Barn at lunch, and I'm not getting involved. I went over there for the snake. You're up to bat this time, Professor.

LIVIE
Damn it.

April 26, 2011

Clary-Smith Clarion
A Covert Faculty NEWSPAPER

Because higher education is a dumpster fire, and we don't have the budget to buy extinguishers

The Clarion has learned that the Board of Directors has initiated an external audit of the university's finances after the affair between Finance Director Karen Reynolds and Athletic Director Champ Rialto was discovered earlier this month. Now they are interested in why the Athletics department has been allowed to overspend so wildly. What a time to join the party.

Word has reached the Clarion staff that the President's secretary has been seen walking through the academic buildings at all hours of the night and day. They are mighty hungry to figure out how this newspaper gets produced and delivered.

For the second time in a week, Officer Boyce Lowder of the Clary-Smith Police Department fell asleep in his car while he should have been catching speeders and collecting revenue in the name of public safety. Several members of the men's volleyball team observed Officer Lowder's slumber, snapped the requisite pictures, and posted them accordingly on social media. For the past year and a half, said volleyball athletes have run a sizable marijuana grow operation in their shared dorm room using an indoor LED light system they stole from the botany lab, and Officer Lowder has been none the wiser. The irony is quite fitting actually.

President McShitface has been observed multiple times this semester hiding in the men's bathroom before faculty assemblies to avoid answering questions. Male faculty members say he sits on the toilet and pulls his feet up out of sight, not realizing they can tell it's him through the cracks in the door. As a reminder, this is the man who collects $196,000 annually—plus benefits and all living expenses—from this institution. Put that in your bong and smoke it with the volleyball team.

Even though she has been on campus for almost a full academic year, Dr. Barbara Cochrane, who came to Clary-Smith from Marion Ridge University in New Jersey last August, still doesn't understand why everybody smiles and waves at her around here.

Back by popular demand, a large vat of Dr. Livie Green's Mamaw's Potato Salad appeared yesterday in the refrigerator of the Yarbrough lounge and it was free for the taking. That tub of creamy goodness did more to lift faculty morale than literally anything the Clary-Smith administration has done in the last decade.

MAY

May 2, 2011

Clary-Smith Clarion

A Covert Faculty NEWSPAPER

Because higher education is a dumpster fire, and we don't have the budget to buy extinguishers

BREAKING NEWS: ENDOWMENT RAIDED
McShitface, Board Poach $20 Million in 4 Years

The Clarion staff are following a breaking story that has rocked Clary-Smith to its core. Financial audits that were just released to SCRAMPI as part of the institution's accreditation process indicate that President McShitface, in concert with the Board of Trustees, has raided the endowment, taking draws in excess of $5 million dollars per year for the past four academic years. This represents an 83% reduction in the endowment's value, a fund that is essentially the only financial safety net the institution has. This outrageous spending now means the university has no unrestricted access to any of the endowment's funds. Stayed tuned to the Clarion for the latest on this breaking story. The faculty have consistently asked about the endowment's status over the last few years, but have been given an epic line of crap in response. The Clarion staff are not sure where transparent answers are to be found, but we are on the hunt.

***

"All right, in our next class we will talk about Marianne Moore's quirky little poem, 'A Jelly-Fish.' Be sure to read the Moore bio in your anthology, and study the poem using the literal/figurative close reading strategy we have been working with. And Kenny, can you stay after class for a minute?"

"I think I know what this is about, and I am so, so sorry. There's no excuse," Kenny said once the classroom cleared out.

"You are such a good student, Kenny," Livie said. "Why in the world would you sleep in my class?"

"This is not an excuse, but my dorm doesn't have any air conditioning," Kenny explained. "As soon as the weather turned hot, I started having trouble sleeping at night. I can't even focus in my dorm to study. I have to go to the library where it is cool so I can think."

"Ah. I see," Livie said. "I'm sorry to hear that the dorms are making it difficult for you to function. That's really not fair. I know it's the end of the semester, but do your best to stay awake in your classes."

"Yes, ma'am. I am actually transferring to UNC Wilmington for next year," he said.

"Well, that will be a great loss for Clary-Smith. I have certainly enjoyed having you in my class."

LIVIE
I have "A" students sleeping in the back
row of my seminar classes because
they can't sleep in dorms with no AC.

ROGER
What I don't get is how the university can
possibly justify having a college dormitory
with no AC and then having the gall
to charge students the same amount
of room and board as the students
living in the more updated dorms.

MERYL
There is no way we will retain those
students. I mean climate control is a
basic necessity at an institution that
charges $25,000 a year.

LIVIE
Oh, we are losing them. This student
is transferring to UNCW.

ROGER
Shit.

To: AllFaculty; AllStaff
From: Forsythe, Keesha
Sent: Mon 5/2/11 9:01 a.m.

May is National Stroke Awareness Month, so it is important that we all review the signs of a stroke in order to be prepared in case of emergency. The sooner a stroke victim receives treatment after symptom onset, the better the long-term prognosis.

It is time to seek medical attention if you experience:
- Dizziness
- Trouble Speaking
- Vision Changes
- Weakness in Your Arms
- Confusion
- Facial Drooping

To Good Health,
Keesha Forsythe, RN
Clary-Smith School Nurse

To: Forsythe, Keesha
CC: AllFaculty
FROM: Ponsonby, Georgiana
SENT: Mon 5/2/11 9:10 a.m.

Keesha,

It is the last week of classes before final exams. Everybody on this campus is incredibly busy––except you, apparently. We have endured a whole year of your emails about sunscreen, broccoli, jumping jacks, and all manner of other topics that relate in no way, shape, or form to our actual jobs. We're tired. But it sure as shit is National Stroke Awareness Month, so by all means, let's email about it.

Sincerely,
Dr. Georgiana Ponsonby
Associate Professor of English, Clary-Smith University

To: Ponsonby, Georgiana
FROM: Harper, Denny
SENT: Mon 5/2/11 9:15 p.m.

Dr. Ponsonby,

We need to have a discussion about the email you sent to Keesha Forsythe this morning. Please come to my office today at 4:00 p.m. for a chat.

Denny Harper
Human Resources Director, Clary-Smith University

ROGER
It's my turn for plagiarism.

MERYL
Oh Rog.

ROGER
I was just grading a student essay,
and it was about to get an A. I was so
jazzed. And then I flipped over to the
last page, which contained the receipt
where the student had bought the
paper online.

LIVIE
How do the ones who make this
decision come to class and look us
in the eye knowing how much we
want to help them succeed?

GEORGIANA
Well, with Rickles in charge of
the Honor Board, let's hope you
actually put "Students are not
allowed to buy papers on the
Internet" on your syllabus.

ROGER
I DID!

LIVIE
Hahahahahahaha!

DENISE
Well done, sir.

May 3, 2011

Clary-Smith Clarion
A Covert Faculty NEWSPAPER

Because higher education is a dumpster fire, and we don't have the budget to buy extinguishers

For several weeks, the Clarion staff has been hearing from reliable sources that more cuts to the Humanities programs are imminent, though no specific program names have emerged. The next victim, unfortunately, is now clear. It's Art. This administration is systematically gutting the Humanities in the name of austerity while simultaneously spending like a sugar daddy on the Health Sciences. Every single program closure has felt like a sucker punch, but the end of the art program just might be too much to bear.

The Business department's annual colloquium, which brought in leaders from all over the county for a week of events, is finally over. Colloquium meetings were scheduled in the library's reading room without notifying the librarians, all of whom had to scramble to reschedule six prior research appointments and a Friends of the Library event that had been on the calendar for three months.

The Yarbrough Humanities building was originally constructed in 1890 but was last updated in 1932—as America emerged from the Great Depression. Students taking classes in room 115 now know that they can't sit on the right side of the room when it rains because the roof leaks. See. They're learning—no matter what the Dean of Assessment's assessments say.

The business office is planning to release a new check request form that will be implemented into their procedures with the start of the new fiscal year in July. We have not seen a draft of the form yet, but we have total confidence that you will not be able to complete it correctly, so be prepared for all manner of scolding.

If you didn't already have reason to love Tammy Jane Hillyer, this will push you over the edge. Last week she told a board member that Grim couldn't come to the phone because he was almost through with a really hard puzzle, and he insisted that he not be disturbed for any reason.

To: Alder, Dutch
FROM: Green, Olivia
SENT: Thu 5/5/11 8:03 a.m.

Hey, Dutch. I just saw the Clarion article about the art program being on the ropes. I am so very sorry. There are no adequate words to describe my feelings about what this school is doing to the Humanities.

If it is any consolation, I heard about a job that you would be PERFECT for. My friend is the city manager over in Hickory Grove, and within the next few days, they will be posting a job listing for a City Arts Director. The first major project will be to commission ten murals on the sides of buildings that line the new walking trail they just opened. After that, the job will transition to things like public school outreach, searching for a new gallery space to host visiting artists, and coordinating the art vendors of the Silver Queen Corn Festival. These are all things you would be brilliant at, and you wouldn't even have to move. If your salary is anything like mine, this job would be a 50% increase. If you are interested, send me your CV. I can make sure you are the frontrunner before the job posting is even listed. We have to get you out of here and into a better situation.

Dr. Olivia Green
Associate Professor of English, Clary-Smith University

To: Green, Olivia
From: Alder, Dutch
Sent: Thu 5/5/11 8:10 a.m.

Livie,

I didn't sleep at all last night. I stayed up applying for jobs all over the country just like I have been for the past two years. It's just so demoralizing. Your message, however, gives me a glimmer of hope. Thank you so much for thinking of me. I will send my CV in a few.

Dr. Dutch Alder
Clary-Smith Art Department (All of It–It's Just Me)

May 6, 2011

Clary-Smith Clarion
A Covert Faculty NEWSPAPER

Because higher education is a dumpster fire, and we don't have the budget to buy extinguishers

Artful "Raiders of the Lost Endowment" political cartoons have been popping up on the inside of bathroom stall doors all over campus. The pieces feature McShitface as a drunken Indiana Jones with fistfuls of cash. We don't know who is responsible for them, but please accept a "well done" from the Clarion newsroom.

The Budget and Finance Committee has approved a whole fleet of new athletic vans. We already have a fleet of athletic vans, and they are in pretty good shape. On the other hand, we also have exposed wiring in the stacks of the library, so yeah. Cool.

The senior music recitals were an astounding display of talent and hard work. Not a single administrator was in attendance, though. Instead, they were all at the grand opening of the newly renovated Exercise Science labs, an event which can only be described as an administrative group bang. They do love to throw parties and congratulate themselves for the many ways they resource the health sciences.

If you haven't yet noticed, Admissions is desperate for incoming students. At this point it appears that any human with even an intermittent pulse will be eligible for scholarship. Get ready to dumb it down even further next year.

Finally, IT Help Desk Director Misty Lineberger is really leaning into being as unhelpful as she possibly can. Her most recent email to faculty with her instructions for setting up their new voicemail inboxes actually included the phrase, "I hate to even say this, but if you have any questions, let me know." This is just the disposition we were looking for in someone whose *whole job* is to help people.

To: All Humanities and Sciences Faculty
From: Grim, Ronald
Sent: Fri 5/6/11 3:01 p.m.

Colleagues,

We need to schedule our final Humanities and Sciences meeting of the year. Let's do Monday at 11:00 a.m. in Yarbrough 108. See you then!

Dr. Ronald Grim,
Dean of Humanities and Sciences, Clary-Smith University

To: Grim, Ronald
CC: All Humanities and Sciences Faculty
From: Alder, Dutch
Sent: Fri 5/6/11 3:07 p.m.

Dr. Grim,

The faculty are in the middle of the final exam period. We are grading papers and administering tests right now. Can we develop an alternative plan that would prevent us from having to attend a meeting?

Dr. Dutch Alder
Clary-Smith Art Department (All of It—It's Just Me)

To: Alder, Dutch
CC: All Humanities and Sciences Faculty
From: Grim, Ronald
Sent: Mon 5/9/11 8:16 a.m.

Dr. Alder,

I am just now seeing this message. We are still meeting this morning because there is business we must attend to before the semester ends. I am looking forward to seeing you all there.

Dr. Ronald Grim
Dean of Humanities and Sciences, Clary-Smith University

5/9/11 Humanities and Sciences Meeting Minutes

NOTETAKER: GEORGIANA PONSONBY, DUCHESS OF ETERNAL GRUDGES
IN ATTENDANCE: 19 FACULTY MEMBERS
LATE (AS ALWAYS): DR. NOAH CAREY
IN ATTENDANCE BUT GRADING PAPERS: ALL OF US REALLY
PRESIDING: THE DEAN OF NOTHINGNESS

11:01 a.m. The Dean of Nothingness admits "there is not much on the agenda."

11:02 a.m. The collective rage is palpable in the room. This is toxic.

11:04 a.m. The presentation slide is stuck. Tammy Jane Hillyer is summoned to assist because this man has never successfully troubleshot anything in his entire adult life.

11:10 a.m. Dean of Nothingness announces the Dean' Council will be traveling to Colonial Williamsburg for a planning retreat this June. Faculty are reminded by Dutch Alder's group text message that the university is in danger of not making summer payroll.

11:13 a.m. Dean of Nothingness suggests that this meeting time could be used to "reflect on our successes this year."

11:14 a.m. The Humanities and Sciences faculty refuses to reflect. End stop.

11:15 a.m. Dean of Nothingness claims the semester has "wrapped up as far as what I need from you." Not a single person in attendance believes that (including Tammy Jane Hillyer).

11:16 a.m.	Denise McGillicuddy stares with glazed-over eyes at the wall. Right on schedule, 9 months of being knocked around in the Grimball machine has broken her.
11:19 a.m.	Communications professor Dr. Allison Barkley has a silent panic attack thinking about how much she has to do between now and graduation. She darts out of the room to splash cold water on her face and hyperventilate properly in the ladies room.
11:21 a.m.	Feeling the poisonous energy in the room, the Humanities and Sciences faculty decide to commandeer the meeting. It's a full-on mutiny. The "Questions from the Floor" part of the program commences.

1. "My reimbursement from last semester has not been paid. When will there be money?"
2. "Where does the investigation into Champ Rialto, Karen Reynolds, and the university's finances stand?"
3. "What is the plan for rebuilding the endowment? Will the Board of Trustees be held accountable for their mismanagement?"
4. "The Admissions Department provides weekly enrollment updates to the senior leadership, but that information is rarely shared. What are the latest projections as of this week, and what is the average GPA of the incoming class?"
5. "Why is the Public Relations

Department not promoting the
Humanities?"

6. "When is the university website going to
be updated? The 'Christmas at Clary-
Smith' banner is still at the top of the
main page."

7. "The Admissions counselors are
promising several majors to prospective
students that do not exist, and students
aren't realizing it until they get here.
What is going to be done to stop this?"

8. "Is it true that the administration is
considering the addition of a football
team? Do they know how many millions
of dollars the start-up will cost?"

9. "Is there any chance that the university
could pay for the Camp Wish Makers
Fall Service Trip in lieu of picking up the
wine tab at the upcoming Deans' Retreat
in Colonial Williamsburg?"

10. "Do you anticipate it will be June or July
when you increase our fall class sizes
without telling us?"

11. "Is it true that the Finance Planning
Committee forgot to include the cost of
paving the parking lots in the budget for
the new Master of Science in Nursing
building and that the project is now an
additional $250,000 in the red because
of it?"

12. "Instead of hiring consultants for the
Fall Faculty Conference, can we develop
workshops that are meaningful to our

own work? The money we save could be put back into our programs."

13. "When will our retirement match be restored?"

14. "How is the Clarion so right about everything? Is the administration any closer to figuring out who is responsible?"

15. "Your answer to the previous question wasn't really an answer. When will our retirement match be restored? It is a benefit that we were contractually promised as a condition of our employment."

16. "Should we apply to present at conferences in the fall, or is professional development money permanently gone?"

17. "We need a specific SCRAMPI accreditation update. Who is completing which parts? Where do we stand with it?"

18. "Can you confirm that the basketball locker rooms will be remodeled before the exposed wiring in the library stacks will be repaired?"

19. "Was the golf cart that Tripp McLovelace ran into the lake ever recovered, or is it still down there?"

11:52 a.m.   In utter exasperation, the Dean of Nothingness adjourns the meeting. That's another year of complete fruitlessness in the books.

May 9, 2011

Clary-Smith Clarion

A Covert Faculty NEWSPAPER

Because higher education is a dumpster fire, and we don't have the budget to buy extinguishers

BREAKING NEWS: Fire Destroys Historic Garringer Gazebo

Saturday's Clary-Smith Honor Society induction ceremony was marred by tragedy when the unity candles that had just been lit by the inductees began to shoot sparks, catching the fraternity's banner and then the 198-year-old Garringer Gazebo on fire.

Following an investigation, the fire marshal ruled defective wicks in the candles (purchased by the club from Becky McLovelace's Pretty Perfections artisanal candle company) were the cause of the blaze. In addition, the fire marshal's report noted that several of the ingredients used in the candles acted as an accelerant that caused the blaze to intensify once firefighters arrived. At least one firefighter was treated at the scene for inhalation of toxic fumes.

First constructed in 1813 by the deaf children of the Garringer School, the precursor to Clary-Smith University, the gazebo originally stood on the southern side of campus. It was moved to Troy Lake and restored through a historic preservation grant in 2007 when its original site was razed for the construction of the Lucas Rude Health Sciences building.

When reached for comment about the conflagration, art professor Dr. Dutch Alder, who spent the unpaid summer of 2006 writing the historic preservation grant that saved the structure four years ago, said, "What in the actual fuck, man?" After the Clarion reporter gave him a few minutes to process the news, he responded again with, "What in the actual fuck, man?" No further comment was available at the time of publication.

To: AllFaculty
FROM: Hines, Peter
SENT: Tue 5/10/11 9:37 a.m.

Faculty

, Your finl grades are due in the Registar's office by Thursday at
12:00 p.m. May 12, 2010, in a vanilla envelope with your name
on the tabs/

Peter Hines
Clary-Smith University Registrar

May 12, 2011

Clary-Smith Clarion
A Covert Faculty NEWSPAPER

Because higher education is a dumpster fire, and we don't have the budget to buy extinguishers

BREAKING NEWS: Clary-Smith Soccer Team Wins Divisional Championship, Rialto Fired for Sexual Misconduct

On the very day that the Clary-Smith Men's Soccer team won the divisional championship and punched their ticket to the national playoffs, Athletic Director and Soccer Coach Champ Rialto was fired by the university. Due to the language barrier, the *Clarion* staff needed the help of Spanish professor Elena Crisp to seek comment from members of the team. Most of them were confused about what had happened because, as one of them put it, "We thought Ms. Karen was Champ's wife."

To: AllFaculty; AllStaff
FROM: Grim, Ronald
SENT: Fri 5/13/11 12:59 p.m.

Colleagues,

Just as a reminder, faculty are required to attend the graduation ceremony in the Keith Gymnasium. It is a mandatory attendance event. The deans will have sign-up sheets, so we will know who attends and who skips.

Dr. Ronald Grim
Dean of Humanities and Sciences, Clary-Smith University

GEORGIANA
Yeah, we'll see how mandatory it is
for the business faculty. The ones with
dicks are playing golf in Hilton Head
this weekend.

MERYL
They just hired that one woman
to teach the Business
Communication course because
teaching writing was beneath them.

LIVIE
Gag.

Clary-Smith University
Commencement Exercises

Saturday, May 14, 2011 10:00 a.m.
Byron O. Keith Gymnasium

Processional	Dr. Beth Hollins (piano)
Invocation	Rev. Fitzgerald Duval
Welcome Address	President Grady McLovelace
Valedictorian's Address	Jazzmyn Sykes
Greetings from the Deans	Dr. Ronald Grim
Tarracino Student Service Award	Provost Gloria Taylor
Excellence in Teaching Award	Provost Gloria Taylor
Musical Selection	Clary-Smith Concert Choir
Keynote Address	Dr. Aki Sato, Professor of Mathematics, N.C. State University
Awarding of Degrees	Peter Hines
Conferring of Degrees	President Grady McLovelace
Benediction	Rev. Fitzgerald Duval
Recessional	Dr. Beth Hollins (piano)

GEORGIANA
Okay, we are an hour into this cluster of a ceremony. So far nobody has been handed a diploma, and the keynote speaker hasn't even been introduced. There is no way my bladder is going to hold.

ROGER
I'm a recovering Catholic. I say with certainty that nothing needs to be any longer than an Our Father.

LIVIE
And how about that Excellence
in Teaching Award going to
Dr. Henrietta Davenport.

GEORGIANA
A dean who hasn't taught a class
in more than twenty years.

MERYL
And who is a complete bully to all of the
junior faculty in the Health Sciences.
She HATES young female professors.
The men in that division get away with
absolute murder though.

LIVIE
You know she forced one of them to
write her recommendation letter for
the award. She's disgusting.

GEORGIANA
My eyeballs are floating. I know
we're not supposed to, but I am
leaving to go pee.

***

"The Duchess of Eternal Grudges, Dr. Georgiana Ponsonby, has contributed a multitude of fabulous ideas since her arrival at Clary-Smith three years ago, but her suggestion that we get drunk after graduation was the best one of all." Meryl Kaiser, who had only been inebriated a handful of times in her life, was so smashed that she couldn't even feel her teeth.

Campus was completely quiet. The last of the graduates and their families had departed hours before, and all of the dorms sat empty, many of them so severely damaged from parties that it would take Lester and Brent the whole scalding hot summer to get them back into shape again for August. There were more stars in the clear sky than any of them had seen in a very long time.

"Roger, are you wearing your rockstar undies today? Hahahahahaha!" Georgiana was lit up and sprawled out in a most undignified fashion in one of the chaise lounges on top of the chapel.

Roger didn't answer. He was a tiny bit passed out for a second.

"When is frigging Fitz getting here with the cigars? I need to smoke," Georgiana wailed.

"He'll be here in ten," Livie said. "But listen, don't y'all push him to drink when he arrives. He takes the church's request that he not imbibe very seriously. I have a lot of respect for that. And he can't stay. He's preaching in the morning."

"Oh, of course," Denise said, sipping a sparkling water and taking her responsibility as the designated driver very seriously. "I can't believe this place is here. You totally can't see it from the ground level."

"That's the beauty of it all," Livie explained. "We come up here once or twice a week to vent. We all need a place to go nuts."

"Well, I think we should take this opportunity to begin our Clary-Smith summer detox by verbalizing our grievances and thus releasing them," Meryl declared.

"I'm here, I'm here," said Roger, regaining consciousness.

"Welcome back, doodoo brains," said Georgiana cackling.

"I'll go first," Denise said. "Three weeks after the fall semester started, Grim called me into his office to confront me about why all of my office hours were in the morning. I had to explain that I teach every afternoon. When he was finished, I went to the bathroom to cry and call my mom to talk about quitting."

"He wouldn't let me go to my uncle's funeral," Roger chimed in. "The week after that, he came to my book release party in the library, which seemed nice, right? No, it wasn't. He got up and walked out ten minutes into my presentation, took a book off the sales table, and didn't pay."

Georgiana now had the hiccups and asked for a pass.

"I don't think I told y'all," Livie offered. "I kicked his ass a few weeks ago in a formal faculty senate grievance about my performance evaluation. He criticized my pedagogy for being outdated even though he has never observed me teaching."

"He stopped by my office at the end of last semester when I was racing to get a giant stack of papers graded and asked why I was so stressed out. He said we should find some paper-grading software to do that for us," Meryl said.

"He was the chair of the promotions committee when I went up for associate professor last year," Georgiana explained. "His feedback to me was that 'We will give you the promotion to associate professor this time, but we really don't think you will ever have what it takes to be a full professor.'"

"Yeah, they gave you promotion, like you didn't earn it. And by their estimation, there is nothing you could do in the next six years before your eligibility for full professor to earn that promotion. What a sleaze," Livie said in disgust.

"After Fitz gets here with the smokes, let's go ride around," Georgiana suggested.

"Hells to the yeah," Roger added.

"That's cool," said Denise. "I can drive your drunk behinds around. The back of my van is full of the twins' baseball gear, though. You'll have to sit among six bats, multiple pairs of cleats, and a bucket of balls."

***

"So where are we going here, people?" Denise asked as she pulled out of the chapel parking lot. "I don't know these roads all that well yet. Duchess, put that bat down before you bust out my back window."

"Give me that," said Meryl, taking the bat from her.

Roger was in and out of consciousness in the back seat, wearing a catcher's face guard.

Livie was riding shotgun with the window of the van rolled down. It made her feel really free to have the warm summer air blowing in her face. Being with her favorite people on the chapel roof tonight had made her thankful that she had such amazing friends. She realized how much their relationship with each other kept them all sane and strengthened the department. In that moment, she was really proud of all they had achieved this year and of the number of ways they had helped students. Hearing her beloved colleagues recount their grievances also made her incredibly angry. She had done everything humanly possible to protect them, but that didn't lessen her frustration when the university's garbage managed to leak on them anyway.

Then it hit her. "I know exactly where we're going," Livie said. "Turn here."

To: AllFaculty; AllStaff
FROM: The Clary-Smith Board of Trustees
SENT: Mon 5/16/11 8:00 a.m.

The Board of Trustees is sad to share the news that Dr. Grady McLovelace, Clary-Smith's fifteenth president, will be leaving his post effective immediately to enter into retirement and spend more time with his family. The Board will host a reception to honor his accomplishments at a later date.

Due to his distinguished service as Dean of Assessment for the last 12 years, Dr. Varner Earnhardt has been awarded the honor of serving as interim president while a search committee is formed.

Finally, it is with a heavy heart that the Board of Trustees announces the closure of the Art program. No teach-out is planned for remaining art majors, though discussions are ongoing about the possibility of hiring an art adjunct to teach a drawing class in the fall.

MERYL
I mean golly.

DENISE
Does anybody know anything?

LIVIE
Word among the chairs is that something bad happened Saturday night at a donor dinner. That's all I've got.

ROGER

It was a matter of time. The
real headline is that they gave
the interim job to good old Varney.

GEORGIANA

Boy these bastards just
fail up, don't they?

DENISE

Has anybody checked in with Dutch?

LIVIE

I did this morning. He's not
okay, but he's trying hard to be.

ROGER

What does all of this mean for
the English program, Livie?

LIVIE

I don't want to go so far as to say that we're
safe, but we do have a level of security in the
number of General Education classes that we
teach. The admin would have to restructure
Gen Ed requirements in a way that probably
wouldn't pass SCRAMPI muster to actually
get rid of us. Our major could be eliminated,
but they have to have us to teach first-year
writing and Gen Ed lit courses.

May 17, 2011

Clary-Smith Clarion
A Covert Faculty NEWSPAPER

Because higher education is a dumpster fire, and we don't have the budget to buy extinguishers

BREAKING NEWS: McShitFace Canned After Public Urination

Despite the Board of Trustees's claim that President Shady McShitface voluntarily stepped away from his post to "spend more time with his family," the Clarion staff has learned that he was actually fired so he could spend more time with a team of rehabilitation specialists at a chic detox center in Palm Springs, California.

According to our well-placed sources, it all started Saturday night at Ruth's Chris in downtown Wilmington, where McShitface was entertaining several potential university donors. He apparently was already intoxicated when he arrived for the meeting, and the 40-ounce ribeye he ordered was not enough to soak up the slosh in his gullet and provide any sobering effect.

Sources claim that by the time the additional drinks consumed during dinner had taken full effect, McShitface was hammered. As hard as his dinner guests protested, he insisted with equal force that they come out and see the waterway, the Riverwalk's premiere attraction. That is where he dropped his trousers and took an actual piss in the river, all while extolling the "freeing virtues of whizzing outside."

A nearby Wilmington Police Department officer observed McShitface in the act and cited him for indecent exposure and public urination—both misdemeanors.

The potential donors, of course, decided against signing a check for the university. We think we speak for everyone in saying that if we had seen McShitface's pecker against our will, we likely wouldn't want anything to do with Clary-Smith either. Hell, we work here, and we really don't want anything to do with it now.

LIVIE
Just so y'all are aware, our contracts
expire on May 18. That means three
glorious months of being able to ignore
the dean's emails.

GEORGIANA

DENISE
The freedom of summer.

GEORGIANA
You know he will try to take a steaming
dump on us at the last minute.

MERYL
Of course. And he will only have Tammy
Jane to push around this summer.

ROGER
I forgot. She is on a 12-month contract.

LIVIE
She is. Fitz keeps her on the
church prayer list because of it.

***

GEORGIANA
Livie, I sent my final edits to the last
Clarion issue to your personal email.
It's ready to go.

LIVIE
Perfecto. I will get them printed
when I am in town today and hand
them off to Lester and Brent for
delivery tomorrow. Another great
year of stellar journalism in the
books. Happy summer, Duchess.

GEORGIANA
Yes, queen.

***

LIVIE
Can I stop by your office this
evening and make photocopies?

CARTER
Sure thing. That school is going to fire
you when they figure out what you're
doing with that newspaper. And what
with Mama being in such a delicate
state because of the church scandal,
one more thing is liable to kill her.

LIVIE
That's some heady talk from a man who
never intends to marry or have children
even though his Mama is counting on it.

May 18, 2011

Clary-Smith Clarion
A Covert Faculty NEWSPAPER

Because higher education is a dumpster fire, and we don't have the budget to buy extinguishers

The Clarion staff members find it poetically just that after a solid year of reporting about the institutional calamities that have befallen Art Professor Dr. Dutch Alder, we finally have happy news to share. He doesn't work here anymore. Effective June 1, 2011, Dr. Alder will be the new City Arts Director in Hickory Grove, NC. Furthermore, he locked into a base salary that is a 60% increase from his Clary-Smith salary. He has also been given his own office that nobody can take away and the budget to begin searching for a community gallery space that can host large art shows and public art classes. We will miss you, Dr. Alder.

As was expected, the demise of the historic Garringer Gazebo due to the fire caused by Becky McLovelace's candles also marked the demise of Pretty Perfections, LLC. We hear that her decision to close the business and dispose of her remaining stock in the hazardous waste site at the landfill was strongly encouraged by the fire marshal. With her husband in inpatient substance abuse rehabilitation in California, her attentions have now turned to a new venture: Precious Perfections, Purveyors of Fine Mesh Ribbon Wreaths, LLC. When you go to the craft store looking for a career, this is what happens.

Nobody really pays much attention to them, but the service center on campus logged 89,706 service hours this academic year. It's an incredible achievement, and we celebrate it.

Dr. Ronald Grim, the Dean of Humanities and Sciences, was the victim of an unfortunate vandalism event sometime on the night following graduation. The hooligans apparently used baseball bats to pulverize his mailbox. No word on motive, and local police don't seem to have any leads.

The lacrosse team is in search of a new captain, as Tripp McLovelace has decided not to return to Clary-Smith for his fourth attempt at his freshman year and has instead decided to focus on the paid internship at American Bank in uptown Charlotte that a Board of Trustees member secured for him. That assistance helped him get past that pesky little background check issue too. Best of luck, Dipp. And to the entire American Bank organization, you are in our thoughts and prayers.

To: All Humanities and Sciences Faculty
From: Grim, Ronald
Sent: Thu 5/19/11 11:30 a.m.

Colleagues,

As we wrap up another successful academic year, I need your help in finalizing a few minor loose ends.

1. Please send Tammy Jane Hillyer copies of your final exams. We need them to be on file to stay in compliance with SCRAMPI.

2. I need a list of everything you have done this year: all the classes you have taught, the conferences you attended, the campus events you attended or organized, the committees you served on, the public service you completed, the student clubs you advised, the publications you produced, etc.

3. I also need you to look back at the calendar of professional development events that were offered this year and provide an accounting for which ones you attended.

4. Please update your curriculum vitae and email it to me.

5. I need several volunteers to teach summer classes. They start tomorrow, so let me know as soon as possible.

6. All administrators will participate this summer in the 360-degree evaluation process. Later today, Tammy Jane will email you a link to a questionnaire that will allow you to evaluate my strengths as an administrator. The activity should take about two hours to complete.

7. Last fall, Human Resources sent me an email about a requirement for everyone in the division to complete a customer service training module that will help us be more accommodating to students. The email got lost in my inbox, and the deadline is tomorrow. Please complete that by 5:00 p.m. It should take three hours. Tammy Jane will email the link.

Dr. Ronald Grim
Dean of Humanities and Sciences

To: Grim, Ronald (AUTOREPLY – OUT OF OFFICE)
From: Green, Olivia
Sent: Thu 5/19/11 11:31 a.m.

Dr. Olivia Green is out of the office for the summer while she embarks on the "unachievable" goal of finishing her novel. If you should have any questions about the English program before she returns in August, please message Dr. Ronald Grim, the Dean of Humanities and Sciences, at rgrim@clary-smith.edu. Send him all kinds of messages. He will be delighted to respond.

Dr. Olivia Green
Associate Professor of English, Clary-Smith University

ABOUT THE AUTHOR

Dr. Ashley Oliphant is a retired full professor of English, an author of five books, and a professional speaker who travels all over the country presenting on her research specialties, which include American writer Ernest Hemingway, fossil shark teeth, and the New Orleans pirate Jean Laffite.

Her college teaching experience in North Carolina offered her twenty years of fulfilment and included stints as a chair, a program coordinator, a service center director, and a writing center co-director. Her teaching duties focused on twentieth-century American literature, literary modernism, Hemingway's novels and his connection to the outdoors, first-year composition, and English language history. She owes a debt of gratitude to the wonderful students, colleagues, and mentors who made her journey so worthwhile.

Oliphant earned her doctorate in English from the University of North Carolina at Greensboro in 2007 with a dissertation entitled "Hemingway's Mixed Drinks: An Examination of the Varied Representation of Alcohol Across the Author's Canon" in which she advocated for a close textual reading of references to alcohol in Hemingway's fiction, one that is not clouded by the author's own biographical connection to drinking. She is also the author of *Hemingway and Bimini: The Birth of*

Sport Fishing at the 'End of the World', a text that explores Hemingway's big-game fishing exploits in the western Bahamas in the 1930s, and his contributions to the formation of the International Game Fish Association. Oliphant has been published in the Hemingway Review, and she has presented at the Hemingway Society's wonderful conferences.

In 2021 Oliphant released *Jean Laffite Revealed: Unraveling One of America's Longest Running Mysteries* with co-writer Beth Yarbrough. The mother-daughter team used primary documents and artifacts to prove that the pirate Laffite faked his death in the 1820s, hid in Cuba for a time with the help of some influential friends, and then moved back to the United States using an alias. He died in North Carolina in 1875 at the age of ninety-six. Their discoveries rocked Laffite studies and opened up incredible new avenues for scholarly exploration.

Oliphant is also the author of *Shark Tooth Hunting on the Carolina Coast*, the only full-color guide to fossil shark tooth hunting in the Carolinas. Published in 2015, the field guide has sold more than twenty-thousand copies.

Writing fiction has proven to be a wonderful counterbalance to the rigors of Oliphant's research-intensive nonfiction projects. In 2018 she published *In Search of Jimmy Buffett: A Key West Revival*, a book that introduced the world to heroine Livie Green—an associate professor of English who has had quite enough and quits her job in the middle of a semester to move to Key West. *Higher Education: Chronicles of a Dumpster Fire* is the prequel to *In Search of Jimmy Buffett*, and follows Livie through her final academic year before she wisely decides to go on walk-about and reclaim control over her life's trajectory.

Oliphant's retirement from higher education has afforded her the opportunity to teach in a variety of other satisfying ways. She offers summer camps and interactive fossil experiences for children interested in learning about shark tooth and seashell identification. She also teaches adult studies courses and leads shark tooth hunting field trips. Her full schedule on the national speaker circuit keeps her busy as well.

Oliphant splits her time between the piedmont and the coast of North Carolina where she leads a very happy life with her husband Chris, son Miller, and cats Schooner Wharf and Irish Kevin. Her lifelong dreams are to own a signed first edition of Hemingway's *The Old Man and the Sea*, to find a whole junonia seashell, and to meet Jimmy Buffett.

CPSIA information can be obtained
at www.ICGtesting.com
Printed in the USA
JSHW021242260723
45397JS00006B/176